MAKING GOOD LOVE TO A BAD BOY 3

BREANA MORGEN

Copyright © 2019 by Breana Morgen

All rights reserved.

No part of this book may be reproduced in any form or by any electronic or mechanical means, including information storage and retrieval systems, without written permission from the author, except for the use of brief quotations in a book review.

❁ Created with Vellum

AUTHOR'S NOTE

Hey! I can't believe we're at part three of this series already! By now, you're probably feeling as though these characters are a part of your everyday lives – at least that's how I feel writing them! You're probably mad at a few of them, in love with a couple of them, and rooting for some of them to win. My personal favorites are: Domino, Bailee, and that darn Davion. Yes, I know he's a butthole, but what eighteen-year-old boy isn't at times? He just needs a little...guidance.

This book, as all my others, is dedicated to so many people. You ready for this list? God – thank you for giving me the gift of writing. I enjoy making people laugh, cry, think, and fall in love with the words I type. Brenyn and Brooke – I couldn't have asked for better daughters. At ages 4 and 1, you two are the biggest influences in my life. Thank you for your patience, your love, your respect, and your heartfelt kisses and hugs. I couldn't do this thing called life without you. Mom – thanks for all you do as a mother and a Mimi. We love and appreciate you, and hopefully we show you just how much on a daily basis. Jiquan – thanks for loving me and all that I come with. I know your job isn't easy, but by now you know it's worth it. Dad – if only you could read this. Thank you for passing along the love of writing to me. Thank you for all you did for me during your time on earth. You will forever live in my heart. I love you; sleep well.

To my readers – THANK YOU! Thanks for your social media likes, shares, and comments. Thank you for purchasing and reviewing my material. With each release, it's my hope to not top the charts, but to give you a story that comes from the heart. Thank you to my publisher, Shvonne Latrice, for your patience, advice, and willingness to always encourage me to believe in my craft. #YouDaBest! And last but not least, thanks to all of my pen sisters under Shvonne Latrice Presents! You all encourage me, make me laugh, and are there for me when no one else can understand the stresses that can sometimes come with this industry.

I hope that everyone reading this enjoys this story as much as I enjoyed typing it. I'm excited to hear your thoughts, so please don't hesitate to leave a review and/or reach out to me on social media. Happy reading!

SOCIAL MEDIA HANDLES:

Facebook: Breana Morgen
Facebook Groups: Breana Morgen's Book Spot and In Reverie Publications
Instagram: @bee_emdoubleu

OTHER BOOKS BY BREANA MORGEN:

Revenge Is Sweet 1-2

Between The Sheets: A Compilation of Erotic Valentine's Day Tales

Addicted To You: A Twisted Urban Romance 1-2

Making Good Love to a Bad Boy 1-2

Chapter One
BAILEE RODGERS

Standing in front of me was the very last bitch I wanted to see. She was smiling deviously as hell, which let me know she'd come to start shit. Popping her gum and standing with her hand on her hip, she opened her mouth to speak, but I beat her to it. The last thing I had was time for her this morning.

"What the hell are you doing here, Tatianna?" I began pulling my hair into a high bun, because I just knew I was about to have to fight.

"I came to celebrate opening night! After all, you didn't think you could leave the manager out, did you?"

I had to roll my eyes at that shit, because Domino told her ass to stay in Columbia and hold it down while we were here. He was going to flip his shit when he saw her, because that meant nobody was there to manage the club in his absence.

Speaking loudly as hell, Tatianna continued. "Did you happen to forget about our little deal, Ms. Rodgers? Just wondering, because I haven't heard from you. Hopefully you've gotten with your man and convinced him, because you're running out of time." She tapped her rose gold Michael Kors watch just as Domino walked up behind her.

"Convinced me of the fuck what? Tatianna, what's your stupid ass doing here, and Bailee, why the fuck you look like that?"

I knew my face was flushed; I could never hide my emotions. I was hoping Tatianna had forgotten about her little threat from a couple of weeks ago, but obviously, she was serious.

Domino was getting impatient, I could tell. So, I spoke up, before he got agitated with me over this hoe's actions. "I don't know what she's talking about, baby. But, I think she was just leaving."

Tatianna threw her head back in laughter, and it took everything in me not to stomp her ass through the floor. "I was afraid you'd try to play this game, Bailee." She reached into her clutch and pulled out her phone, but before she could find what she was looking for, Dom snatched it.

"What you looking for in here? I'll find this shit for you, 'cuz y'all pissing me off with this dumb shit. It's motherfucking six thirty in the morning and y'all bit – *females* – wanna be starting shit."

"Give me my phone, Domino!"

I guess he wasn't fighting too hard to keep it, because Tatianna got it back. "*This* is what I was trying to show you."

"It's a picture of Bai. I don't see a dick in her mouth or in her pussy, so get the fuck out my face." Domino walked into our room, and I took that opportunity to try to slam the door on Tatianna's messy ass, but she pushed me back hard as hell, making me fall on the floor.

"She's leaving the abortion clinic in that picture, Domino! This was a few weeks ago! She aborted your baby!"

My chest got tight as hell. I got dizzy, nauseous, and scared. I couldn't move. My palms started sweating, and I was so lightheaded that I felt like I was going to pass out. I reached out for Domino's hand, but he slapped it back. "Is that shit true, Bailee?" He roared loudly, with fire in his eyes. I'd never seen him so angry.

I opened my mouth to speak, but no words came out. Even if I wanted to lie, I couldn't, because since Tatianna had an iPhone, I knew the date, time, and location of the picture were on her phone as proof.

"Domino. Baby. Let's talk about this, okay? We can talk in private."

Ignoring all the tears in my eyes, he whipped out his phone. When I heard him requesting to change my flight to an earlier one, I knew he was pissed. I just hoped I hadn't lost him.

Tatianna stood in the doorway snickering, and although I wanted to punch her in her mouth, I had to take responsibility for what I'd done. After all, she didn't make me go get an abortion – she just used my situation to her advantage.

I begged Domino to talk to me, but he remained silent as he packed up my clothes and sat them outside of the hotel room. I'd never seen him so calm after hearing bad news, and that's what scared me the most. We'd always been able to bounce back after disagreements, but I wasn't sure if this time would be the same. I just couldn't accept the fact that my mistake could've caused me the love of my life.

Before leaving the hotel room, I yanked Tatianna by her raggedy Brazilian weave, and knocked her head against the door, making her wide ass nose bleed. "Bitch!" I spat in her face. "That's for being in my motherfucking business!"

I heard Dom chuckle when her body dropped to the ground, but unfortunately, he didn't call my name to come back. As badly as I wanted to run back in that room and beg him to take me back, I had to have some dignity about myself, and own up to what I did. I hurt him, and I just prayed that one day, he'd find it in his heart to forgive me.

Two weeks later...

It's been a rough fourteen days, and I honestly don't know if I can go fourteen more. Not like this. Everything in my professional life was going great – I now had steady clients at school and the money was coming in handy, since I no longer had Dom supporting me. Don't get me wrong, I could hold my own, but it was nice having a man around to wine and dine me. Now, I had no one to even do the simplest of tasks, such as rub me down after a long day, or kiss me to tell me I'm beautiful, despite my morning breath and bed head. My love life sucked.

After Domino paid for my flight to be changed to an earlier one, and then paid an Uber to take me to the airport, I didn't hear anything else from him. I was selfish as hell in my decision; I'll admit that. But, his silent treatment was the ultimate punishment, and I didn't know if I could stand it even longer.

When I got back from Miami, he was still down there, yet all my shit was packed up in boxes on his porch. I'm guessing he called and told the same secret service ass niggas that always came to pick up bodies to have my things sitting outside. I took that as a sign that he really didn't want anything to do with me, so as bad as it hurt, I packed my car and called my girl Celine. I've been staying in one of her extra rooms since then.

What's crazy is that normally, after an argument, I'd block Domino from calling me, but this time I didn't. I wasn't mad at him. I wanted him to call me, just so I could explain and ask for his forgiveness regarding the abortion. He hasn't. No text, no inbox on social media...nothing. I constantly checked my phone, hoping one of my calls, texts, or emails was from him, but every day I was thoroughly disappointed. It got to the point where I now hated when my phone rang, because I knew it wasn't him. I wouldn't have even known he was alive if I didn't stalk him on social media. I've reached out to him several times, but all my texts and calls go unreturned. I even called him off Celine's phone, and when he heard my voice, he immediately hung up.

I wanted to see him so bad that Friday night, I even went to The Black Palace in hopes of seeing him. I didn't even get inside the door. I walked around to the back door, and it was locked. It was as if he'd predicted I was going to come try to talk to him, so he made sure I had no access to him. The only thing I hadn't done was go to his house, and that was because I feared not only rejection, but embarrassment. What if he was with another girl already? My heart wouldn't be able to take that. So, I've decided to spare myself the agony, and stay away. I firmly believed if he was meant to be mine, it would happen. I guess the wait was just the hardest part.

No, I lied. The hardest part was saving face for my family and friends at school. The only people that knew what was going on between us were Celine, Janay, and Camiyah. My parents didn't even know I wasn't living with him anymore. The girls at school didn't know either. Everybody thought we were the perfect couple, and the truth is that we were. Are. I just have to make him realize it was a mistake. But trying to get someone back is kind of hard when they won't talk to you.

Celine had been begging me to move on, but what she didn't get was that I could meet ten other men today, and altogether they still wouldn't equate to the man I'd lost. Just because it was easy for her to get over Davion didn't mean my situation was the same. I mean, Davion was an ass. They didn't have anything real. Dom and I did. But, I couldn't get that through to my hard-headed ass friend. She was so adamant about me finding my happiness in someone else that she'd gone behind my back to set up a blind date with one of Eric's friends. And that's why I was now getting dressed, although I really didn't want to. It wouldn't hurt to get out the house, but I hoped he wasn't banking on this going anywhere. Because unless his name was Domino Black, I wasn't interested.

"You look good, chica! Jason is gonna love you." Celine walked in giggling just as I'd finished curling my hair. I had parted my hair down the middle and put large, loose curls in it. This was the first time I'd attempted to do anything for my appearance since leaving Miami. On the outside, Celine was right – I looked pretty damn good. But on the inside, I was miserable.

Once I finished curling my hair, we headed to the steakhouse where Celine had made our reservations. I'd never been on a blind date before, and I wasn't looking forward to it. Blind dates seemed so juvenile, and meeting someone new was pointless. I wasn't in the mood to start over. Dom knew everything about me – my favorite color, my favorite foods, how to reach my g-spot, my fears, my dreams, my failures... just the thought of having to share that with someone else made me want to vomit. Having to open up to someone new... introduce my family to someone new...learn what someone new liked in bed...none of that appealed to me, despite how great of a guy Celine claimed this Jason character was. He wasn't Domino.

"There they are." Celine pointed to Eric and a guy who I assumed was Jason, sitting at a table set for four. Just from glancing at him, I could tell he was attractive and well-dressed, but I still wasn't interested. Maybe in another lifetime...

When we made our way to their table, both Eric and Jason stood up to help us into our seats. Then, Jason introduced himself to me.

"Nice to meet you, Jason. I'm Bailee." I extended my hand, and he kissed it. *Sweet.*

Not knowing what to say after his gesture, I just half-smiled and replied, "Thanks" and took my seat next to him. My first impression of him...handsome, but like I said, he'd have to be...

"Is that Domino?!" I blurted out, louder than I meant to. Patrons beside me stopped eating for a second, just to look over at me. Nosey asses.

Embarrassed, Celine shook her head. "No, chica. It's not."

I'd been doing that. Way too often. Thinking I saw him when in reality, it was really someone else or sometimes even no one at all. I guess when the heart wanted something bad enough, it could trick your mind into believing that person was there.

Chapter Two
DOMINO BLACK

That same night...

"Fuckkkk, Domino! Your dick tastes so good, daddy."

"Then shut the fuck up and keep sucking it." There was no point in talking, when all she was supposed to be doing was catching this nut in her mouth.

I palmed the back of this thirsty bitch's head, so her mouth was fully on my dick. Since my shit was large as fuck, a bitch had to open wide like she was at the dentist to fit this motherfucker in, and this hoe was acting scared; my joint was so close to going soft on her stupid ass. She talked a good game, like she knew what she was doing, but the moment I brought her back here to my office, I could tell she wasn't about that life. Typical lil' thot – just trying to get some clout from fucking with me, but her bubble was gon' get popped as soon as I busted this nut. You couldn't get clout if nobody knew you did it, and I wasn't claiming shit.

"Suck this shit. Stop acting scared. It's a dick. It don't bite." I didn't even know this damn girl's name, nor did I care. I wasn't wifing her. Shit, I wasn't even taking her number, because I had no plans of talking to her past today. I just needed her to catch this nut so I could go about my fucking day. I was backed up and I needed a fucking release.

I spilled my seeds in her mouth, and instead of swallowing my shit like the pro she tried to portray herself to be, she spit it out. Amateur. Bailee would've swallowed and then begged for more.

The lil' thirsty hoe stood up, smiling like she'd actually done something. Little did she know, I'd only busted that nut because I put thoughts of Bailee in my head so I wouldn't go soft. I was imaging her sexy, full lips wrapped around my joint, making those moaning and gagging noises she always made.

"You want my number? Maybe we can do this again."

"I sure fucking don't, and we sure fucking can't." I pulled up my jeans, waiting on her to exit my office. But, she just stood there like she was fucking retarded. Looking like a passenger straight off the short bus. "Your legs broke?"

"No."

"Then move them bulky motherfuckers. Shave 'em while you're at it. Get the fuck out of my office."

"How could you talk to me like that?"

Easy.

Ignoring her dumb ass question, I opened my office door

and waited for her to walk out. When she finally did, I slammed that motherfucker behind her and locked it, 'cuz she seemed like the type to try to come back in. I needed some time to myself, and Weezy was handling everything out on the floor so I could go through emails and shit. I fired that bitch Tatianna after the shit that went down in Miami, only because she clearly had a motive and I still hadn't figured out what it was. But any motherfucker who sits on information and then takes a damn trip just to deliver it when they're ready, has a motive. And I wasn't one to have disloyal motherfuckers in my camp.

Scanning email after email, I saw one from that bitch ass singer Tony Marshall's people about throwing a party here after one of his concerts coming up. The answer was hell to the nah, so I deleted that motherfucker and went to the next. I'll be damned if I had a nigga in my spot who was trying to fuck with my girl. And before you try to correct me, yes, Bailee is still my girl, even though I ain't fucking with her right now. Anybody who thought I'd just let her go didn't know me very well. Nobody was getting any of that good pussy juice except me. She just had to learn a lesson, and until I felt she was ready not to fucking go behind my back with shit, she was cut off, and I was doing me.

A hard ass knock interrupted me from my thoughts about Bai, and I frowned, wondering who the fuck would be crazy enough to act like the damn police. I grabbed my gun in case I had to blow a motherfucker's head off. "Who dat?"

"It's me…Camiyah."

I put my gun back in the drawer and opened the door for her. "If you ever in yo' hoe ass life knock on my door that hard again, you'll be left with no damn hands."

She walked in and sat her sweaty ass in my chair, but I shook my head and motioned for her to get up. "We ain't that fucking cool. You might be Baby D's bitch, but you ain't mine. Stand yo' ass up."

I heard her huffing and puffing and shit, but I bet she got the fuck up out of that seat.

"Here." I handed her a wad of cash equaling five hundred dollars. She came in here the other day, showing me a paternity test proving Baby D was the daddy of her funky ass baby, so since it was looking like that nigga would never man the fuck up, I'd been throwing bread her way almost every day, just to make sure the baby had diapers and shit. I also let her get her job back, but I told her she had to lose a lil' weight. My joint wasn't gon' be known for the strip club with dancers looking like busted cans of biscuits.

Smiling like she'd just won the lottery, Camiyah took the cash and stuffed it in her bra. Well, her shirt; I don't even think she was wearing a bra. And if she was, she needed to take some of that money I just gave her and get a new one ASAP.

"Why yo' titties dragging the floor? Perk them motherfuckers up before you bring your ass back in here to dance, alright?"

Trying to push those low motherfuckers up, she smirked and sucked her teeth. "Well, if you must know, your niece sucks me dry. But, I will. I have a special bra that should do the trick. And that's *if* I come back in here to dance. I'm still not sure yet."

I didn't give a damn what she decided, because her pussy being in the air here wasn't a favor to me. Moving onto other business I had with her, I asked, "So what's going on with Bai?"

I told Camiyah to keep an eye on her for me, since they got kind of close in Miami. She'd been reporting to me on her whereabouts and shit. The other night, I broke into Celine's crib since Camiyah told me Bai was staying there. I wanted to see if I caught her in bed with another nigga, but she was sleeping peacefully as fuck by herself, so I left. When I checked her panty drawer, there wasn't any scent of sex on any of them, either, so I knew she'd been behaving herself.

"Nothing. The usual, I guess."

"What the fuck you mean you guess, Camiyah? I guess I'ma have to stick my foot up your ass, huh?"

She smirked and shook her head. "Domino. She's not messing with anybody, okay? Bailee ain't doing shit but moping around over you."

"But has she learned her lesson?"

See, real shit, I wasn't tripping over the abortion. I'm sure bitches I've fucked with have had abortions in the past. I didn't care about them or their damn babies. With Bailee, I was so mad because we were supposed to be better than that. There wasn't shit she was supposed to be able to hide from me. That shit had me thinking that if she could hide something big like my baby from me, she couldn't be trusted. And I didn't want to feel that way about my shorty, 'cuz I fucked with her heavy. After Sapphire, I didn't trust no bitch until Bailee, so I was all fucked up in the head over this bullshit. Since I was the type of motherfucker that didn't give trust easily, after that shit was broken, it was hard as fuck to repair. Damn near impossible.

"She certainly did." Camiyah nodded her head as she answered my question. "She wants you back, Dom. She's sad all the time. Crying all the time. Please call her."

"I will. When I'm ready. You can let yourself out."

She didn't run me. No female did. I'd holler at Bai when I was good and ready, but until then, she'd better not even let another nigga think he had a chance, or else his blood was gon' be on her hands. All I needed her to do was keep going to those expensive ass classes I paid for, and sit in the house and think about how she would never do that selfish shit again. And of course, have that pussy nice and wet when I did decide to fuck with her again.

The next day...

When my boys and I linked up, that shit was a fucking problem. None of these hoes were safe; it ain't no fun unless the homie could get some, right? The Black Palace was open for business, but my niggas, Terrell and Roman, were with me in one of the back rooms, letting some of these bitches dance for us while we drank and smoked away our stresses. Terrell had some shit going on with his baby's mama, and Roman was bitching about wanting Janay back from Weezy, but what he didn't know was that those two were close at fuck now, so he didn't stand a chance. Weezy was here, but he was holding down the club for me, but he was popping his head in every few minutes, probably hoping to get some of the action. If I were that nigga, I'd stay calm though, 'cuz Big Lena could come bust in at any minute, and he knew damn well he could never win against her. That's why he was still staying at my fucking crib.

"Can I bust it wide for you, Domino?" One of the stripper hoes that had just gotten hired here named Princess, asked as she sat on my lap, straddling me, ready to do her thing. She was sexy as fuck, too. Not as sexy as Bailee, 'cuz nobody was fucking with her beauty, in my opinion. But Princess was a very close second. With skin the color of pecans and jet-black smooth hair, she looked like a Barbie doll…well, if stripper Barbies was a thing.

"You sure can." My dick rose, but I wasn't fucking her. Not because I didn't want to, but because I had no protection on me, and for all I knew, her pussy might've been as infected as Charlie Sheen's dick. Rule number one – never fuck a stripper raw.

During the dance, she kept whispering in my ear, asking if I was gon' give it to her. Just to fuck with her, I went along with it, but she was gon' get tossed to one of the homies in a minute.

"I don't want him, Domino. I want you." Princess cooed as

I told her to get the fuck up. I pointed to Roman and told her to suck him off before I considered fucking her. Not that I was planning to hit, though. I was just trying to get my man some action since that nigga was throwing a real life pity party for himself.

"He gon' test you out for me. If he likes the head, I'ma sample the coochie."

"Promise?" She asked, licking her full lips at me as I stood up from my seat. She had no idea I was about to get lost on her ass.

"I don't make promises I ain't gon' keep."

At least I was honest with these hoes.

"I think you meant – "

"I said what the fuck I meant. Gon' over there and fuck with my boy. You wasting my time."

"Okay." She batted her pretty ass eyelashes and walked over to Roman, ready to serve him. Hoe. Even if I was gon' fuck with her, I wouldn't now, 'cuz she'd just shown me she was down to do whatever to whomever. Not the type of female I rocked with. Hoes like her were for everybody, and I wanted my bitch for me only. That's I rocked with Bailee. She might've been selfish, but she was loyal as a motherfucker.

I slipped out the room and went in my office, and I saw I had a missed call from Tatianna. Just as I hit the delete button so I wouldn't hear the message she left me, the door to my office slowly opened.

"So, you were just gonna ignore my call?"

"No. I saw the call. I was gon' ignore the message. Fuck you want, Tati?"

I didn't invite the bitch to sit down, and she knew she wasn't welcomed to, so she stood on the other side of my desk with her arms folded over her tight ass blue dress. "Tati? Are you sure it's appropriate that you call me by a nickname? Bailee doesn't mind?"

She had some strong balls for bringing up Bailee's name, after she whooped her ass at the hotel. Part of me wished Bai would pop up right now just to do that shit again. I needed a good laugh. "Don't get your wig knocked off, alright? Fix that shit, anyway. It's crooked. Fuck you here for, Tatianna?"

She adjusted that ugly ass wig and rolled her eyes. Hell, I wasn't the one who put that shit on her head, so she didn't have a reason to be mad at me. "I'm here to make you an offer you can't refuse. I'm really sorry about what went down in Miami, but it was only because I was trying to build your brand and she wasn't willing to help me elevate you to the next level."

"Word?" I asked, unenthused about whatever bullshit she was about to come up with. I could tell when motherfuckers were talking out their asses, and this was definitely one of those moments. The only reason I let her keep going is 'cuz my eyes were on my emails, anyway. I wasn't listening to this bitch, and had no intention of working with her ever again.

"Remember all those ideas I threw at you, regarding what Mr. Montclair's business can do for you? I still believe we can do this. You need me on your team and I'll make it happen.

I'll make sure that The Black Palace is a household name...if you'll let me help you."

"I won't. That nigga is a snake, and I'm starting to think you're one, too. Get the fuck out of my club, Tatianna." My eyes never left the computer screen, but I heard her take a deep breath and finally stomp off. I didn't know what the fuck her infatuation with that shark nigga was, but she could stop trying to sell his ideas and his brand to me. I was my own motherfucking brand, and I wasn't the kind of nigga who let motherfuckers dictate how, when or why I got my money, and that's what the old cat was trying to do by having me sign a clause stating his was the only liquor I could serve. Nor was I the type of nigga who let others say that they helped them; everything I got, I hustled for. And it was gon' stay that way. Fuck how anybody else felt about it.

Chapter Three

DEDRICK BLACK

Ugh, life. I just...I just don't know anymore. One minute, I'm okay, and the next, I'm full of rage. I think when Brittany hurt me, she woke a sleeping giant. I didn't even know who I was anymore. I felt bipolar. I knew I was depressed. And I didn't know how to get out of this funk. I wanted to be happy, but the only thing that made me happy was basking in Brittany's warmth. She was once the Kool to my Aid, and life wasn't sweet at all without her.

Everything about myself, I'd changed to please Brittany, and look where it got me. Burned and alone. My STD went away, but the gnawing in my heart would probably never.

I didn't even feel like playing with my chemicals, so you know I was depressed. I haven't eaten in days, and every night I had nightmares of either my penis burning or Brittany holding my heart and breaking it with a smile on her face, once again. The funny thing is that she was trying hard to get back in my good graces, but I was giving her the silent treatment. It killed me not to know who gave her the black eye she had, but had she stayed with me, she wouldn't have had it. I wanted to protect her and treat her like the queen I presumed her to be, but she clearly wasn't happy with me. I know I'm not the most handsome, or the coolest, or the richest man around, but I was willing to give her the best of me, and it killed me that she didn't appreciate it. Would any woman ever?

I just couldn't believe I'd been so naïve and let her walk all over my heart. I know I should be over it...trust me, I'm trying. It's just that when it's your first experience with love and it ends in you getting played like a darn fool, it's hard to get past it.

Reaching over in my dresser drawer, I grabbed all the pictures I'd accumulated of Brittany over the past few months, and ripped them one by one. I wanted no more memories of her. Maybe if I acted as if she didn't exist, this heartbreak would go away. Anybody who could be that cruel and take so much advantage of someone did not deserve a space in my heart. She was pure evil!

Or, was she? Was it me? Did I come on too strong? Did I do or say something that made her shy away from the love I was trying to give her?

Staring at the pile of ripped photos on the floor, I began to regret it. Now I had nothing to remind me of her. Nothing but vivid memories of the nights I slid into her juicy vagina...

the same vagina that I found out was more like a hot box instead of a wet box. A part of me was happy to have no tangible memories of her, but the other half of me was sad I'd taken such drastic measures. Maybe I should've left at least one photo untouched. Now, I had nothing to stare at as I drifted off to sleep every night...

Lying in bed on my muscle-less back, I began to wonder if the reason Brittany treated me like this was indeed my fault. I couldn't remember a time I'd offended her, but maybe she got hurt by the words Dom said to her in the limo. But, I had defended her every chance I'd gotten, so that should've shown her that I was on her side.

Maybe I showed her through my actions that it was okay to lie and betray me. I didn't have the guidance that most guys had regarding females, so I guess I went about this the wrong way. I should've listened to Domino. He had way more experience regarding women than I did, and although I was praying his jokes and assumptions about Brittany weren't true, they were.

Darnit, Dedrick! You're so stupid!

After my parents' death, I didn't think I could fathom anything that hurt worse. This was it, though. Having your heart broken felt like someone was constantly beating you with a ton of bricks, and the only one who could help was the one who was giving you the beating. Honestly, there was no reason for me to be alive. Whose life did I enhance? No one's. The few people who cared about me were dead, and the one I cared about had abandoned me for the next better-looking, more popular guy, despite my attempts to please her. My brothers laughed at me, not only behind my back, but to my face as well. I had friends who were just as lame as I was, and although I was never bothered before by the words "nerd" and "loser", I did want more out of life. One day, I wanted to get married and have kids and be that world-renowned scientist who cured cancer. But, what good was all the fame and fortune if I had no one to share it with? All my life, I thought my purpose was to cure cancer, or at least to find ways to benefit the earth through chemicals. But, neither of those things could keep me warm at night. Neither of those things would think I was handsome, or assure me that my hair and clothing matched and was becoming of me. Neither of those things would give me the amazing, sensual feeling that Brittany had on those nights she allowed me to enter into her secret garden.

I was such a dweeb, and I was wasting my life while others around me lived theirs. Michael Jackson once said that it was better to be living than existing, and I agreed. At this point, I'd rather be dead than feeling like this.

Grabbing the gun that used to be my father's out of my nightstand, I placed it to my temple and cried. Releasing my anger felt good, but nothing would feel as good as ending my meaningless life.

Chapter Four
BAILEE RODGERS
One week later...

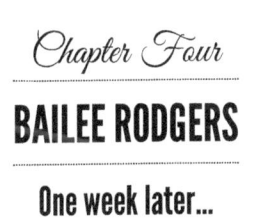

*S*igh. Another seven days without hearing Domino's voice, having the pleasure of his lips against mine, or feeling his fingertips run down the small of my back...but, I was learning to adjust to my new norm. At times, I felt that I'd be okay without him, but during other times, I couldn't do anything but cry.

I'd been talking to Jason just to pass the time, and I'd found out we actually had a lot in common. That didn't make me like him, though. He didn't know it yet, but he would remain just a friend. He wasn't a bad guy at all – just boring, corny, and not at all what I was used to.

Just like me, he'd gone to college because of his parents' wishes for him, but later left, because that's not where his heart was. He then began painting and selling his pieces to art galleries around the United States. Not my forte, but I was proud of anyone who chased their dreams. The only reason I was going to show support, as a *friend*, is because I knew what it felt like to have a lack of support. I wouldn't want anyone to feel that.

"Are you ready, beautiful?"

I wished this nigga would just call me Bailee. Hearing a man other than Domino compliment me sounded weird. I appreciated the gesture, but hearing it from him brought me back to my reality, which was still something hard to face.

"I'm as ready as I'll ever be." I smiled nervously, only because I didn't even want to go tonight. I was only going to get out of the house. Cabin fever is *real*.

Jason took my hand in his, and opened the front door of the townhouse, letting me walk outside first. I felt his eyes scan my body as I stepped out in front of him, which made me uncomfortable. The only set of eyes I wanted gawking over me were Domino's.

"Damn. I'm gonna have the most beautiful date in the room."

This wasn't a date. Or at least, not in my mind.

Nodding my head, I accepted Jason's compliment, because he was probably right. I was most likely not only going to be the most attractive woman there, but probably the youngest, most stylish, and the darkest. He had me going to some art event that I was sure was going to be boring as hell, and I just hoped I didn't sleep through it, because I didn't want to hurt his little feelings.

We were going to the Columbia Metropolitan Art Gallery,

because they'd purchased one of his paintings for a pretty hefty amount. I didn't know shit about art, but I knew that the white folks loved it, and would probably sell their souls for a good painting. And although I wasn't a fan of paintings, I did know that Jason had some pieces that were beautiful, if you were into that type of thing.

Jason opened the passenger side door and let me in. Wearing a mid-length, tight, sleeveless, purple dress with silver jewelry and Balenciaga heels, I admired myself in my compact mirror after buckling my seatbelt. I looked pretty damn good. I definitely looked better than I felt, that's for sure.

A few hours later...

"I had a lot of fun with you, Bailee. Thank you for being my guest of honor."

"Thanks for the invite." I was hoping this nigga would hurry up and leave. Tonight had been boring as hell, and I felt like he was only using me as a trophy. Every time he got a chance, he made it known that I was his date, grabbing my hand and kissing it, or doing something cheesy like spinning me around when there was not even any music playing. Homeboy was trying way too hard. Out of all the "dates" I'd ever been on, this was by far the worse. Saying that I was ecstatic it was coming to an end was an understatement.

"Do you think we can go to another banquet next week?

There's a showing at a gallery in Charleston, and I'd love to have you as my guest."

Hell no. Traveling with this man, even though it was only two hours away, was not my idea of fun.

On the low, I was wondering if he was gay, and trying to cover it up with me. He was nice, but just wasn't manly enough for me. He was extremely particular about things that Dom and other macho men probably wouldn't care about, like his food touching, and his shirt having a small stain. Jason was also soft-spoken, so anytime he got ready to speak, I wanted to vomit. And he seemed too damn eager to take me places with him, as if he had something to prove. I think it's about time we called it quits.

Taking my hand in his, he put my knuckles up to his lips to kiss them. "I'll see you tomorrow, beautiful. Goodnight."

I never agreed to that.

I smiled weakly and took my hand back from him, then closed the door as soon as he stepped on the porch.

"Ouch!" My hair was yanked, but it wasn't hard...just startling. Turning around, my eyes landed on the intruder that had come to get me...

Chapter Five

DOMINO BLACK

"What are you doing here, Domino? Are you fucking crazy?" Bailee grabbed her hair like that lil' pull actually fucking hurt. It didn't. Shit, I'd yanked her shit harder when I fucked her from the back. She was just being fucking dramatic.

"You already know I'm crazy, so why the fuck would you ask me some shit like that, Bailee Rodgers? Who the fuck was that corny motherfucker? Nigga's voice sounded like Janet fucking Jackson. Are you fucking crazy, having some bitch ass nigga dropping you off?" I cornered her, pressing my dick against her middle. That shit was brick hard 'cuz she looked good as fuck tonight. I couldn't believe she was dressed so fucking sexy for a nigga so fucking weak. If she was trying to make me jealous, she'd failed with that nigga. I was just mad she let her pussy in his presence. I thought her standards were higher.

"I thought you didn't want me anymore?" Bai folded her arms like she was mad or some shit, but I knew she was happy to see me. She'd rode past my fucking club enough. The cameras proved that.

After staring at how sexy she looked in this purple dress, I finally responded. "I didn't say I *did* want yo' ass. I know I want one thing." My hand rubbed her pussy through her dress, and that motherfucker was drenched. I'd be lying if I said I hadn't had pussy since I left her alone, but I damn sure haven't had one as wet, tight, or tasty as hers. Bailee's box was unmatched, and that's exactly why she was only giving it to another nigga over my dead body, and even then, she'd better watch her fucking back. I'll fuck around descend from Heaven on her ass, on some "Preacher's Wife" shit.

She tried to move my hands, but I let my fingers creep inside her dress, just so I could tickle her pussy lips. She loved that shit, and I loved feeling how wet she was for me. Her knees buckled, as she let out light moans.

I got on my knees, and began eating that pussy from front to back, until she came all over my beard. By the time I finished sopping up all that good pussy juice, her body was still shaking and shit.

Once Bai had regained her composure, she started back with the questions and shit. "Why are you here, Domino?"

"Because I knew that corny nigga wasn't gon' lick yo' box like I just did. You're lucky I didn't smoke his ass like a turkey, baby. Bringing that nigga in yo' spot and shit." I was getting pissed just thinking about him wanting my girl. If I ever saw that nigga in the streets, I was gon' light his ass like a Christmas tree. Or shit, burn him like Brittany burned Dedrick.

"You're mad at me over what I did to you, Domino, and I know that. You don't want me. I'm a hoe and a bitch, remember?"

She was referring to a post I made on social media about hoes and bitches not being loyal. I wasn't even talking about her, but they say a guilty conscious speaks first. She knew what she did was wrong, and she was trying to make me feel about not fucking with her over the past few weeks, but I wasn't the one who made a major decision without my partner's consent.

Bailee kept interrogating me, and I kept ignoring her ass. I walked right past her and went toward the room I knew she'd been sleeping in. I laughed, looking at all the wigs she had scattered around on the floor. At least I knew she wasn't wasting all her time with that corny nigga – she'd been busy doing shit for school, which is what I needed her to do.

She hopped her ass in front of the door, trying to stop me from entering her room, but Bailee must've forgotten who the fuck I was.

I lifted her small ass in the air and opened the door, then slammed her on the bed, leaning on top of her. "Stop thinking you run shit, Bailee! That's the motherfucking problem! You think I'm mad you got an abortion? Fuck that. I'll put another baby in you right now. I'm mad 'cuz you made the decision alone and had no plans of telling me. I don't do deceitful motherfuckers, but since I know why you did it, I'ma let you fuck with me again. Try it again, and I'm cutting your uterus out."

"*Let* me fuck with you?"

"I said what the fuck I said." I pulled my clothes off and got in her bed. "Come lay down with me. I know no other nigga has been in this bed, so come on."

"And how do you know that?"

I don't know why the fuck her ass liked to try me. She was so lucky she was fine as hell.

I gave her a kiss on the lips before I confessed. "'Cuz I broke in here the other day and sniffed your panties. Next question?"

What the fuck she thought this was? Bai knew I was off my fucking rocker...

Her cute ass was looking at me like I was crazy, so I pulled her into bed with me. I put her on top of me, as I massaged her plump ass cheeks. "Sorry for yelling at you earlier, but I had to put my foot on yo' fucking neck." I started sucking her ear and shit, and I slid my fingers in between her legs where I found her leaking pearl. Inserting two fingers in her opening, I whipped my dick out, flipped her over, and put it in her from the back while I continued to finger her. "I bet you won't try that selfish shit no more, will you?" I was pounding her hard, smacking her ass and pulling her hair with each stroke.

She whimpered and moaned as she shook her head. "No, baby. I...I...I'm sorry."

Stroking her fast and hard, I asked, "You ain't miss me, Bailee? You didn't miss what this dick do to you?"

"Yessss! Oh my God, I'm cumming!"

Her juices leaked from her pussy, getting both my dick and my fingers wet, since I'd been double penetrating her. I slid my fingers out of her hole and placed them to her lips so she could taste herself. "See how fucking good you taste? Why you think I'm so crazy over you?" Her shit tasted fruity and sweet as fuck. I could eat my girl's box all day.

Turning around, she stared at me with those big ass, pretty eyes. "I'm really sorry about not telling you about...about everything, baby. I was so scared that – "

"I already know, Bai. It's cool. Just don't do that shit again. Don't worry, we gon' have our baby. Shit, I might've put another lil' motherfucker in you just now. And delete that fuck boy's number, or I'm going to jail for murder, and not for just him."

"Deleting it now." Bailee showed me her phone as she did it.

"Atta girl. You want some more dick?" My shit could go from jello-soft to hard, just by looking at her.

"Let me rest, baby. After all, you did just lay it down."

"You damn right I did. No other nigga could've fucked your cat like that." We chuckled in unison and then I kissed her on those sexy ass lips of hers. After our kiss, she still looked a lil' sad, but shorty had no reason to be. I wasn't mad at her anymore. Camiyah had told me the reason behind the abortion, and that was the only reason I was gon' forgive her ass. Shit, I'm glad she had it, 'cuz had that been Tyler's baby, I would've had to shoot it. But, since it had the potential to be half mine, I still felt like she should've discussed it with me.

It is what it is, though. I haven't always been the best nigga to her, so I guess that was payback or something. I was just happy to have her back in my arms, 'cuz those loose pussy hoes weren't coming close to being able to replace her. Bailee had my fucking heart, man.

A few days later...
I had to go to Miami to check on the club, so my shorty was dropping me off at the airport, with a lil' mug on her face. A nigga was feeling a lil' soft and shit, 'cuz I hated to leave her, but duty called. She wanted all these Brahmin bags and shit, so I couldn't neglect the business that paid me.

As she pulled over to let me out, she let out a long sigh, which was probably supposed to make me change my mind about leaving her. I could tell she didn't trust me because of how shit went down with Tatianna the last time, but she ain't had shit to be worried about. Weezy now replaced that dumb hoe, plus, I was going on this trip alone.

"Dom. I – "

"I already know, Bail. You want a nigga to behave, so that's what the fuck I'm gon' do. You ain't gotta keep telling me.

Hell, I wish you were going, but you gotta hold yo' shit down. I'll be back tomorrow."

She wasn't trying to feel that shit, but she had no choice, 'cuz I wasn't letting her miss another day of school. Only a few more months were left in her cosmetology classes, and I damn sure wasn't gon' be the blame if she didn't finish in time. "What I gotta do? Fuck the attitude up out of you?"

Giving me a half smile, she shrugged and rolled her eyes. "That would be nice. But, baby, we're at the airport."

"Bailee, I know where the fuck we're at. I don't give a damn if we were at church while the pastor was looking us in the face; when I want you, I want you. You telling me I can't have you?" I slid my hand up her dress as my dick bricked up, just to get her kitty ready for me. Removing my fingers from her opening, I sucked on them, enjoying the taste of what was between her legs. "Let me fuck you, baby. You so fucking sexy. Get out the car."

My bitch didn't even object. She just hopped her fine ass out the car and followed me into the closest restroom, where I told everybody to get the fuck out unless they wanted to join. Lifting baby girl onto the sink, I slid up in her as she dug her nails into my back, as I stretched her pussy from front to back, as she whispered in my ear how much she loved me, and never wanted me to leave her. She didn't have shit to worry about. I liked fucking her too much.

. . .

Later that night...

With the business I was in, there was bound to be stupid shit jumping off, but nothing had gone down at either of my locations 'til now. So, when I walked into The Black Palace Miami and saw the police surrounding my shit, I almost lost my fucking cool. Me and the pigs had never gotten along, and I didn't need them snooping around my shit.

The police dogs were out, and all the customers and dancers stood outside, waiting on whatever fucking investigation was going down to be over. A nigga who looked like he was the sloppiest drug dealer ever was getting arrested, and I saw the cops collecting money and shit from the inside of my spot. Considering the fact that this spot hadn't even been in business for three fucking months had a nigga tight; it was hard as hell for niggas to have shit, 'cuz lil' bitch ass niggas like the one in the handcuffs liked to fuck shit up.

The manager I'd chosen for this location, a nigga named Jerrod, hadn't called me about no bullshit popping, but since he was trying to talk to the pigs about whatever the fuck had gone down, I was gon' give him a pass. For now.

"What's going on here, officers? I'm the owner, Domino Black. Fuck happened at my spot?"

"There seems to be a drug ring going on at your establishment, Mr. Black. Tell me what you know about it." The nigga whipped out a notepad and pen like I was about to give him some information. I didn't know shit, but I did know he'd better get the fuck out of my face. Smelling like he'd just fucked a bitch who rolled in Bengay.

Clenching my jaws tightly, I got in his face, just so he'd know not to fuck with me. "You listen to me, motherfucker. I don't know a damn thing about no drug ring going on, but y'all better arrest who you're gonna arrest and get off my premises. I don't fuck with your type and would appreciate it if y'all left this spot the fuck alone."

"Don't let it happen again, Mr. Black." The short, bald fucker handed me a ticket, but I handed that shit right to Jerrod.

"Pay this fuckin' fine, boy." I slapped him upside his head, startling the hell out of him. "If you can't control the crowd, you gon' pay these fines every time."

"I'm sorry, boss. I'll pay it."

After a few more minutes, the pigs and that wack-ass drug-dealing nigga finally left, so everyone went back inside. I scanned the crowded room, happy that the bullshit that had just occurred didn't fuck my money up. Motherfuckers were still coming in here, ass was still shaking, and the bartenders were still pouring.

As I was heading to my office in the back, I felt a pair of hands rub up and down my back. I turned around to see a slim bitch with buck teeth and a body odor trying to seduce me.

"I hear you're the owner. I'm Kayla."

"I bet you did hear, with those damn satellite ears. Get the fuck off me, Dumbo." She was looking hurt, but she couldn't have been anymore hurt than her mom was when the doctor handed her over.

Sucking her butter yellow teeth, she walked away and I headed to my office where I wanted to finally get some peace and fucking quiet. I had no idea that when I walked in my door, I'd be staring at Sapphire, sitting in the chair behind my desk.

"Nice to you see you, Domino."

"I can't say the same. What the fuck are you doing here, bitch? Get the fuck out." In all honesty, Sapph was lucky I didn't knock the taste out of her mouth for being here. It was bad enough that she sometimes showed up at the Columbia spot, but to come all the way to Miami just to bother me, that was some stupid shit.

Walking in my direction, she ran her hands over her breasts and licked her lips as she eyed me. The old Domino might've been turned on, but I just wanted this lying, cheating, stupid bitch out of my presence. I wanted to slap that fucking lace front off her head. The material looked cheap as fuck, like the same shit you'd find on a screen door.

"I know you miss me, Dom." She whispered softly, as her hands roamed my body.

"You must not know shit, 'cuz I damn sure don't." My dick wasn't even getting hard, because it wasn't Bailee touching me. I wasn't attracted to Sapph at all.

"You do. Can we make love, just one last time?"

"I don't know. You gotta ask my girl for permission." I reached in my pocket and Facetimed Bailee, leaving Sapph's mouth wide the fuck open.

As soon as Bai was on the screen, I turned the camera on

Sapphire, and Bail started going the fuck off, just like I knew she would. "What the fuck is going on? Do I need to fly down to Miami to whoop some ass? I will fuck you up, Sapphire!" My bitch was crazy like me, so I knew she wouldn't have no mercy on this hoe.

Bailee was still going off by the time I flipped the camera back on myself. "I just wanted to show you that this bitch was in here, but ain't shit going down. She's musty, anyway. And her lip needs a wax. Nobody's fucking with her."

"Why is she there, Domino? I'm gonna kill you! I fucking trusted you!"

Watching her frown was funny because even though she was mad, she was cute as fuck.

"And you gon' trust me tomorrow, so shut that noise up. Baby, you have nothing to be worried about. My shit still like a gummy worm; wanna see? She came in here trying to fuck me, but I told her she had to ask you for permission. I wasn't gon' hit anyway. I'ma pass her to my dog, though."

"Nigga, you're crazy. Get off my line, and get that bitch out of your office. And Sapphire, when you get back in Columbia, it's on, bitch!"

Click!

I knew Bail was mad 'cuz she didn't even tell me she loved me before she hung up, but at least I'd done my part by proving wasn't shit popping with this bitch. "Sapphire, I don't wanna put my hands on yo' stupid ass, so do me a favor and get the fuck out of my office before I have to beat yo' ass." I didn't have respect for no female except Bailee, plus I had nothing but hatred in my heart for Sapphire, so it was nothing for me to fuck her up. What she did to me would forever leave a bad taste in my mouth.

She finally dismissed herself, but before she made it down the hall, I opened my drawer and called her name.

Coming back inside my office, she smiled. "What is it? You realized that you missed me?"

"Nah." I laughed, shaking my head. "I realized I ain't give you this." I threw some deodorant at her. "Now go in the bathroom and control your sweaty ass glands, and get the fuck on."

Chapter Six
DAVION "BABY D" BLACK

Ever since finding out I was free from all charges for that shit with the dumb lil' underage bitch, a nigga's been on Cloud Nine. I don't know what the hell I'd done to deserve such good luck, but a nigga was on top of the world right about now. Nothing but positive shit was popping for me.

Being back on the field was the best feeling thus far. I'd just finished playing in my first game since my injury, and of course, we won. I was the best quarterback USC had ever seen, so I had no doubt that I would fuck those niggas from Alabama up today on the field. And I did.

"Good game tonight, Baby D. I wish you'd tackle me like that in the bedroom." A white hoe giggled, walking past me with her eyes set on my print. I'd never fucked with a white bitch, but I could only imagine they smelled like wet dogs in bed. And her ass was so flat, that shit looked like a half-done pancake. Nothing I was interested in.

"I'll pass. I can't afford another rape charge." I took a swig of my Paul Masson and laughed as she walked off, mad that I wasn't fucking with her. Becky would be alright, though. And if she wasn't, oh the fuck well. All these bitches could suck my dick. None of them were worth shit; especially one with an ass I couldn't spank.

A few more fans walked up to me and congratulated me on tonight's game, and I signed a few autographs and took some pictures. The bartender had turned on ESPN on one TV and the local news on the other; I was on both, and I was loving that shit. It was about time I got recognized for my athleticism again, instead of all the fuck shit that had been going on. I hated those nosey son of a bitches in my business.

I checked my watch, then chugged back another drink from the bartender as I waited on this nigga who wanted to set up a meeting with me. I didn't know shit about him – just that his name was Jay. Somehow, he got my number, and he called me a few days ago. He told me to meet his ass tonight, in the bar of the Sheraton Hotel at nine thirty, and I'd been here since five minutes before. Usually I didn't wait on people, but this nigga had my interest piqued.

"Are you Davion Black?" A voice behind me asked, as I signaled the bartender to give me another drink. Yeah, I was only eighteen, but everybody around here knew who the fuck I was, so I never got carded or told no. Everywhere I went, they catered to a nigga, which was exactly what the fuck they were supposed to do.

"Is the sky blue, motherfucker?" I turned around to see an old nigga in a big ass Steve Harvey suit and alligator shoes. To set it off, this motherfucker had on a top hat. I laughed right in his corny ass face, but he didn't seem fazed. I pointed at the empty seat beside me. "Have a seat and let me know who the fuck you are, and what the fuck you want." He looked like a fucking magician, but if he said the wrong thing to me, I'd be the one making his ass disappear.

Laughing, he took the seat next to me. "It's not about what I want, Mr. Black. It's about what you want. I've got it."

"And what the fuck would that be?" I was curious. I didn't know this motherfucker from a can of paint, so how could he possibly have what I want? What I wanted was for him to either stop beating around the bush, or leave me the fuck alone. And he wasn't a bitch, so he didn't have pussy, which was the only thing in this world besides coke that I desperately wanted.

Opening his suitcase, he showed me just what he was talking about. Pills. Opioids. Bags of weed. Rocks. You name it, that shit was there. He was lucky the bar was damn near empty. "I told you, young man. I've got what you want."

My pops taught me at a young age that anything that seemed too good to be true, usually was. So I had to ask him what the catch was.

"Nothing." He shook his head, then pulled something out

of his pocket, that looked like a Polaroid. "Just bring him to me."

"And I can have all this?"

"All of this, plus whatever else you want. I'll supply your every need, from now until you're fucking retired from the NFL. Oh and...there's a cash reward for this, too. Would ten grand be sufficient for your troubles?"

I could do a lot with ten g's. Shit, I could do a lot with all the drugs he had in that suitcase. Snatching the picture from this nigga, I wondered how the hell I was gon' bring Domino to him. I don't even think my brother was fucking with me at the moment, so I'd have to find a way to get his ass alone. I wasn't about to miss out on all that money and drugs for nothing.

The next morning...
All night, I thought about whether or not I was gon' bring Domino to that weird nigga Jay. At first, I thought not to, since I didn't know what the fuck he wanted with him. But, the more I thought about it, I realized I didn't owe a damn thing to Domino. My brother was more into pleasing his bitch than he was into pleasing and helping me, so what the fuck did I care about him for?

I didn't owe loyalty to anybody at this point, except Davion. So, if handing my brother over to that creepy ass nigga was gon' take care of me, then that's what the fuck I was going to do. More drugs and money meant a better life for me, and at this point, that's all I was focused on – making sure I was stress free and debt free. And with the way shit was going in my personal life, I couldn't pass up the opportunity to make shit easier on myself, 'cuz shit was rocky as fuck at times. Especially when it came to my personal life.

I don't know what the fuck me and Camiyah were doing, but as bad as I wanted to kick her ass out of my dorm, I refrained, only because the more time I spent with Camia, the more used to her I got. I wouldn't say I liked her or anything, 'cuz I didn't like babies. Or kids. I barely liked people. She was kind of cute, but she was whiny and could be stank as fuck, but I was getting used to having her around. Camia was only annoying half the time; times like this weren't so bad. She sitting in this lil' bouncing shit that Camiyah got her, staring at me as I rolled up a blunt. Camiyah would have a fucking fit if she knew I was smoking around the lil' kid again, but oh well. She wanted to be in my presence, then that's what she'd have to deal with. No matter how cute this baby was, I wasn't about to give up what I loved so much for her. Or her damn mama. Mary Jane calming me down was the main reason I hadn't gone upside Camiyah's fucking head yet.

"Again, Davion? What the fuck?" Camiyah yelled, walking into my bedroom in nothing but a towel. "I leave you to watch her for ten minutes while I shower, and this is what you do?"

"Yep." I blew a cloud of smoke in her direction as she picked Camia up and placed her on her titty. That's part of the reason she was so fucking whiny. Camiyah had her on her titties all fucking day. I blew another cloud of smoke in the air, after inhaling more of my medicine. "And if you don't like it, you can bounce."

"Whatever, Davion." Camiyah's towel fell from her body, and I couldn't front, the jawn was looking better and better nowadays. She'd lost the majority of her baby weight, so she was back to being fuckable again. I wasn't a chubby-chaser, so those rolls had to go. She claimed that was why she kept the baby on her titty all day, but it was probably providing some type of stimulation, 'cuz I hadn't been fucking her. That shit might change, though, now that didn't look a sack of laundry anymore.

Feeling my dick brick up, I reached out my hands for Camiyah. "Come here. Sit on my lap."

"Not with that fucking blunt in your hand, Baby D. Get rid of it. I don't want Camia inhaling weed."

I didn't give a damn what she inhaled, because I knew weed wouldn't kill her. But just so I could get some ass, I put it down. "Better?"

"Yes." Camiyah smiled at me for the first time today, and with Camia attached to her breast, sat her perfectly round ass on my lap. My dick was sticking straight up through my shorts, so she felt it poking her the moment she sat down. "Really, Davion? You want it *now*? The baby is awake."

"Fuck that baby. She ain't gon' stop me from giving you this dick." I sloppily kissed her neck and licked the inside of her ear. I hadn't touched Camiyah in a sexual way in so long that I forgot that between those thunder thighs she actually had some good pussy. That's how she trapped me in the first place.

"Let me put the baby down." She placed Camia on my bed, and her lil' brown eyes were wide the fuck open. Oh well. She'd have to watch her mama get dicked down today.

Entering Camiyah from the back, I pummeled myself inside of her as she belted out a series of 'oohs' and 'aahhs'. I could tell she hadn't let another nigga fuck because her box was gushing wet. Loyalty. I appreciated that shit, even though if she would've fucked someone else, she would've been well within her rights. She wasn't my bitch.

"This my pussy?" I roared, pulling her hair back, as she threw her ass in the air each time I stroked her.

Barely being able to speak, she muttered, "Yes, daddy."

"That's what the fuck I thought. Can I smoke in my own shit?"

"Yes, daddy."

That's what I liked to hear. Having a bitch around wouldn't be so bad if she didn't try to control my ass.

After a few more deep strokes, I felt her juices rain on my dick, so I filled her up with my nut in return. I looked over at Camia and she was watching us fuck, but surprisingly, the lil' fucker wasn't crying. Maybe she was cool after all.

Camiyah led me to the bed and sat beside me, then lifted Camia and placed her in my arms.

"What the fuck you gave me the baby for? Hell am I supposed to do with her?"

Laughing, Camiyah shook her head and rolled her eyes.

"Love on her, Davion. She's yours. *Ours*. She's really a sweet baby, and I want her to feel daddy's love. That's something I never had, and something I know you want back. So, the father Mr. Black was to you...be that to her."

I didn't know if this shit was reverse psychology or what, but Camiyah was speaking some real shit. My pops was the best nigga God ever created, and just knowing I could never be the father he was, hurt like a motherfucker. He was patient. He was funny. Wise. Supportive. My pops was one hell of a man. Every day, I tried to numb the pain of my parents' deaths with pills, weed, and whatever else I could get my hands on for a high, all because I still couldn't accept the fact that they were dead.

Wiping the tears that had fallen from my face, Camiyah kissed me and pointed out that Camia was happy to have me holding her. She was giggling and shit and looking at me with those big, round eyes of hers, and surprisingly, that shit made a nigga feel good inside. "She looks up to you, Davion. That's why I don't want you smoking or doing drugs around her. I don't want her growing up like I did – poor, bouncing from house to house, and with no direction."

"Well, since you're asking a lot of me, I need you to help me with something."

"What is it?" She asked, stroking both Camia's head and my lower back. After the game I played last night, a back rub felt pretty fucking good.

"I need you to tell Bailee we're going on a double date with her and Dom. Soon."

Giving me a weird look, she asked, "Why do you need me to do that? He's your brother. Can't you just ask him?"

"Sometimes Dom fucks with me, other times he doesn't. Just get them to agree to a double date and stop asking me fucking questions. You wanna go out with me, right?" I already knew the answer to that, 'cuz I'd never taken the hoe outside of the house, except for when we went to Miami. She smiled and nodded her head, confirming that she wanted a date with me. Shit, who wouldn't?

"Okay."

Just for agreeing to do what the fuck I'd asked, I gave her a kiss on the lips before handing the baby to her so I could head to practice. Part one of my plan was officially in effect...

A few hours later...

The sound of my phone vibrating woke me from a deep sleep. I'd fucked the shit out of Camiyah, but I'd tired myself out too. And whoever the fuck this was blowing my damn phone up was gon' get cursed the fuck out if this annoying ass baby woke up.

Extending my arm across Camiyah's naked body, I grabbed my phone and saw that all the vibrating was coming from Instagram. I didn't know who the fuck PrincessOfBelAir was, but she was damn sure hitting my inbox hard. I hated profiles without a fucking picture up. I never answered messages from those sketchy accounts, but the message caught my attention.

PrincessOfBelAir: I miss you, baby. I'm so sorry. Let's get past this.

Me: Who the fuck is this?

PrincessOfBelAir: Shanay, baby. I can explain. I just wanted you to love me. I'm sorry I lied about my age, baby. I just want us to be a family. I had a dream the baby is a boy.

I didn't give a fuck if it was five boys in her belly; they didn't have shit to do with me. After taking a screen shot of the messages, proving that this psycho ass hoe was reaching out to me, I blocked her account and put the phone under my pillow.

Less than five minutes later, before my black ass could even close my eyes good, my shit vibrated again, but this time it was a text from my teammate, Josh. He sent me a video and when I opened it, I instantly got mad as fuck. The lil' bitch Shanay had apparently just leaked a sex tape she'd made of us, on social media. I wouldn't have given a fuck if it was anybody else, but since this bitch was underage and I'd just beat these fucking charges, I didn't need all this shit resurfacing. A nigga just couldn't win, huh? I unblocked that fucking Instagram account she'd just written me from, sent her a long ass message, cursing her the fuck out, and put the phone on silent, so I wouldn't be interrupted anymore tonight. I was sure the video was gon' have the news back talking about my ass, and I just hoped that like everything else, the shit blew over quickly. As far as Shanay, that bitch was dead to me, and she better hope I never saw her or her baby, 'cuz they were both liable to get fucked up. Causing me all these fucking problems!

Chapter Seven
BAILEE RODGERS

I was so happy Dom was coming back home today, because I'd been anxious as hell to share my good news with him. I hadn't even told my girls yet, because I wanted my man to be the first to know. Earlier today, I found out I'd been chosen by my instructor to do a showcase next Saturday. The winner of the show is set to receive a check for five thousand dollars, which I could use to go towards the down payment for my shop. When I graduate, I really don't want to work in anyone's salon but my own, so this competition was really important to me. I felt like God and the universe were placing me exactly where I needed to be.

Pulling up to the airport, I spotted Domino from a mile away. His sexiness exuded from his head to his feet, and he couldn't get over here fast enough so I could hug and kiss all over him.

"Damn, baby. You really missed your man, huh?"

The moment he got close to the car, I'd hopped out and damn near jumped in his arms. It felt so good being back in his presence, because staying at the house last night and sleeping alone drove me crazy. Since he wasn't there, Weezy had stayed with Janay, and the house was too fucking big for one person. I missed his arms being wrapped around mine, and I missed that chocolate dick being available to me in the wee hours of the night.

Dom placed his bag in the backseat, and as soon as I pulled off, I told him the exciting news. "Baby! I'm gonna be in a showcase next Saturday, and if I win, I get a check for five thousand dollars! All I've got to do is do two styles – one on a woman and one on a man, showing my skills!"

Hearing the words roll off my lips got me even more excited. It seemed too good to be true!

"A man? The fuck you gon' do on a nigga's head? He better be one of those gay motherfuckers."

Out of all that I'd just said, this fool was just worried about the fact that I'd have to cut or do a man's hair. *Jealous ass.*

"Actually I don't know who the people are, but I have to do creative styles on them in like forty-five minutes, and the judges will decide the winner. You're gonna be there, right babe?" I couldn't imagine doing it without him.

"Coming to bust a cap in any nigga's ass that looks at you the wrong way." He spoke so nonchalantly, like he didn't just threaten a person's life. This nigga was crazy.

"You act like you didn't just have your ex bitch in your office last night," I reminded him. I was still livid at the fact that Sapphire had made her way down to Miami to see him, and I couldn't help but wonder how the fuck she knew he was there. Rage took over me as I pushed my foot against the gas and sped to pass the slow moving car in front of me. I was getting pissed just thinking about Sapphire being in my man's office.

Dom's dramatic ass gripped his seatbelt. "What the fuck is yo' problem, Bailee? Don't you wreck this shit, girl."

It was *my* car. Yes, he bought it, but it was mine.

I pulled over in the median and threw the car in park. "How the fuck did Sapphire know where you were, Domino? And you better answer my question!"

"I don't know, wanna call and ask her? Come on with yo' crazy ass. I got something to give you."

I knew he was talking about dick, but as much as I wanted to feel him inside of me, I was going to refrain until he explained to me why she knew his location. Or at least until I smelled it.

Reaching into his pants, I whipped out his erect dick and sniffed it as he laughed.

"My joint don't smell like shit but Dove soap, right?"

"And it better stay that way, nigga." We chuckled in unison and after he promised me that he hadn't had any contact with Sapphire, I decided to drop it. Didn't want my man feeling like I didn't trust him.

. . .

A few days later...

In order to prepare for the showcase, Dom had gotten me some mannequin heads, so for the past couple of days, I'd been practicing not only at school, but at home too. Tonight, Camiyah was coming over, so I could get some practice in on her head, and also so we could have some girl talk. We'd been so busy with our men and everything else going on that we hadn't had time to hang out lately. Dom would be at the club tonight, so I was looking forward to some drinks and chick-flicks with my new friend.

"Damn! This house is nice as hell!" Camiyah shrieked when I let her inside. Our house was the fucking bomb, but it wasn't the biggest I'd ever seen. Camiyah, on the other hand, probably thought Dom's four-bedroom, three-bathroom home was a mansion, since she was used to Section 8 housing.

After getting to know her, she let me in on her upbringing, so that's when everything started to make sense – the stripping, chasing after Baby D, and the clothes she wore. She was starting to look better, though. In Miami, homegirl was cute when we went out, because she wore clothes that she stripped in, but during the day, her t-shirts were dingy, and her jeans had holes in them. Tonight, she looked much better.

After hugging and giving her a quick tour of the house, we settled in the kitchen where I'd prepared us a light dinner consisting of barbecue flavored chicken drumettes, deviled eggs, mozzarella sticks, and fresh fruit. While mixing our margaritas, she began to let me know all the details I didn't care to hear about regarding her and Baby D's newfound relationship.

"He's so different, Bailee. I swear. It's like, since he realized Camia was his, he's trying to be a better man for me and for her."

I didn't believe it for one minute. Niggas like Baby D didn't change; they just knew how to act when they wanted something.

She must've read my expression, because she was trying so hard to convince me. "I'm so serious. I think we're really working it out."

"That's nice." My tone was probably dry as hell, but that's because I was so skeptical. One minute, Davion acted like a normal citizen and the next, he was back to being an entitled fool. She was better than me for dealing with his shit, and I prayed he never did anything to harm the baby. He was so temperamental.

After we ate, I washed her hair and then we went into one of the guest bedrooms, which Domino had made into a little salon for me.

"This is so dope, Bailee."

"Yeah, it is, isn't it? All Domino's idea." The room had a salon chair, a sit-under dryer, and a variety of hair products and tools. My favorite was my Chi flat iron, because it got my hair and everyone else's bone straight.

"Domino seems like a really good guy for you, Bailee. I'm happy for y'all. I hope Davion and I reach the level y'all are on one day. Domino should teach him some things."

Chuckling, I shook my head as I began to towel-dry her hair. "He's tried, girl. Everybody has. Baby D does what the fuck he wants to do and it's sad, but he won't fully grow up until something happens to knock him off his high horse."

"I think we should go on a date; like a double date. Just so that maybe we can all talk some sense into Davion. It seems like we can all have a good time together. I mean, Miami wasn't that bad, was it?"

Miami wasn't bad at all, but we weren't double dating in Miami, either. I wasn't required to be around Davion if I didn't want to be. Yes, we partied together, but that was it. A double-date? I wasn't too sure how this would play out. Just the thought of having to be around Davion while he disrespected her at a dinner table disgusted me.

Just so I wouldn't hurt her feelings, I agreed to ask Dom about it, before changing the subject. He tolerated his brother but not more than he had to. For obvious reasons. And I couldn't promise that my mouth wouldn't stay shut if anything were to be said out of line.

Night of the Showcase...

I was a nervous fucking wreck, staring at everyone in the audience. The show hadn't started yet, but me and the other stylists were all set up on the stage. The judges sat on the front row, and not one of them wore a smile across their face. The audience was hyped though; surprisingly, my parents and my sister were in attendance.

I also spotted Celine and Eric a few feet away, and Camiyah sitting in the back. Janay had to go dance at a party tonight, so I knew she wouldn't be here. The one person I wanted to see the most was nowhere to be found. Domino.

The emcee for the show stepped to the front of the stage, and as he spoke into the mic, a group of ladies walked out and stood beside us. I figured they were our models. A few seconds later, a group of men followed suit, and I almost peed on myself when I saw that the male model coming to stand beside me was Domino.

"What are you doing?" I whispered, as my knees buckled, just from staring him in his deep almond eyes. My cheekbones were hurting from smiling so hard. Leave it to Domino to make my moment even more nerve-wrecking...

"I told yo' ass you weren't gonna be doing shit on no nigga's hair besides mine. I'm the only muse you need." He sat down in the chair in front of me. "Cut it. And don't fuck my shit up." Luckily, the tools we were provided with included clippers and razors, because otherwise, there wasn't a damn thing I could've done to him.

I wasn't sure how the hell he'd maneuvered his way past security or even convinced everyone backstage to let him be my hair model, but I was glad he did. Having him on stage made me much more comfortable, and cutting his hair and trimming his beard was easier than I'd expected. I guess because I knew how I liked my man to look.

While the judges made their decisions, Dom squeezed my

hand tight. "You got this, baby. And if you don't win, I'm shooting this motherfucker up."

The crazy thing about it was that I knew he was serious.

"And the winner is...Bailee Rodgers!" The emcee read my name off the envelope, making me almost have a heart attack.

I saw my family and friends stand up and cheer, then the entire audience followed suit. Dom walked me to the front of the stage, where I received my five-thousand-dollar cash prize; I was one step closer to getting my own salon, and although I'd done all the work, I couldn't have done it without my man's encouragement and his presence. Today was a good day, and Dom didn't know it yet, but tonight was going to be a *very* good night for him.

Chapter Eight
WEEZY
The next day...

I'd asked Domino if I could take a day off, just so I could spend time with Janay and handle some shit that I needed to with my lawyer. I was finally planning to divorce Lena so I could finally move on in peace with my new shorty.

"Are you sure you're ready for a divorce, Weezy? I know with the kids and everything, it's a big decision to make." Janay stared at me with those mysterious, light brown eyes that made a nigga hard on sight.

We were eating lunch at Red Lobster, then I planned to take her to meet my mom. Shit was already serious between us, in my opinion, but once I filed for this divorce, shit was gon' get real. I'd never been excited for a female to meet my mom before – the only one she'd met so far was Lena. So I hoped by having Janay meet my mom, she'd realize how serious about her ass I was. First, I wanted her to change her clothes, though. So, I was taking her shopping. That was my next surprise for her. I felt like if she was gon' be around my mom, she needed to be dressed just a little more appropriately. Shit, I wished I could throw her entire wardrobe away, 'cuz I didn't approve of damn near any of the clothes she had, now that she was my woman.

Don't think I was one of those controlling niggas, 'cuz I wasn't. Lena had that on lock, and I wouldn't dare do the shit she did to me, to anybody else. I wasn't the type of nigga who tried to change my woman, either. I accepted people for who they were, regarding their physical appearance. I mean, shit, look at Lena. I never asked her big ass to lose weight. The only thing I wanted to do was take Janay shopping, so she could get some better shit. I wanted her to not only meet my mother in better clothes, but also dress classier whenever she was or wasn't around me.

My issue with Janay's clothes was that I hated she left nothing to the imagination most of the time. True, she danced for money, but she also had an honest job and was a college student. She didn't have to dress revealing all the time.

I don't know, man. Maybe I'm feeling like this because I really liked her. Any other hoe, I wouldn't give a fuck about. But if Janay was gon' be my woman, I didn't want no other niggas knowing what she had. It was bad enough that she danced for 'em. That shit would have to end, sooner than later, too.

"Weezy? I asked you a question, baby." She waved her hand in front of my face, bringing me back to reality.

I nodded my head and smiled, as she asked me once again if I was ready to leave Lena. "I'm ready for a divorce. Been ready. And the therapist thinks I'm ready too." Between having a good woman, a good therapist, a steady job, and no drugs in my system, I was really able to think clearly. And the truth was that I should've left that abusive relationship a long time ago. I reminded myself of my mom so much that it was crazy, but my therapist was helping me work past that shit. I hadn't realized how fucked up on the inside I really was until I'd started seeing a shrink.

"Well, if you're sure you're ready, then I support you." Janay squeezed my hand and continued to eat her shrimp scampi. "What are we doing the rest of the day? I have a test to study for later, but I'd like to get some more time in with you. I'm happy you took the day off."

"I gotta go by my lawyer's office later. But, I wanna take you to meet my mom. Think you ready for that?"

Her eyes lit up like a Christmas tree. That was so fucking cute to me. Other than Lena, my mom hadn't met anyone. When I was fourteen, she caught a white girl giving me head in my room, but other than that, -I kept bitches away from my family 'cuz that shit wasn't serious. Some niggas I knew introduced every hoe they fucked to their family, but not me. I was a mama's boy for sure, and you had to be special to meet her.

"How is your mom going to feel about you dating me, knowing you're still married?"

I laughed and shook my head, busting open my king crab leg. "My mom ain't gon' give one fuck, two fucks, a red fuck, or a blue fuck about that shit. She can't stand Lena." My mom despised Lena, since she was the same way toward me that my dad was toward her. Hell, she'd be happy as fuck to know that I moved on. She'd been begging me to move in with her for years, but my pride wouldn't let me. "I do want you to do me a favor, though."

"Anything for you, babe."

I was glad to hear that.

"Let me take you to the mall and buy you something to wear. You know, some shit that doesn't show all your skin. I want you to start dressing with a little more class."

"Are you saying I have no class, Renard?" Her voice got loud, and the nosey motherfuckers at tables around us looked over.

"Ain't no fucking show to see here. Eat your goddamn food." I spat at them niggas, then focused my attention on baby girl. "That's not what I'm saying. You just don't leave enough to the imagination. And being my girl...I don't want to have to slit a nigga's throat for thirsting over you. That's all."

"You've been around Domino too long," she laughed. "I get it, though. I just can't really afford much besides these cheap, hoochie clothes. I get these little dresses on sale at Rainbow for like ten bucks. Anything else is above my budget.

All my money goes to my mother for bills." My girl started looking all sad and shit, making me feel bad. So I got up and sat right beside her, putting my arm across her shoulders as she cried softly. I hated seeing her like this, and I could kick my own ass for even bringing the shit up.

I kissed the top of her head, hoping to make her relax a little. "It's okay, baby. I get it." I understood what it was like to work and have no money for yourself. Shit, before I moved out, when I did work, my money went straight to Lena's bank account. She'd gone online and changed my direct deposit information behind my back, then when I confronted her about it, she blacked my fucking eye. Then, when I got my unemployment checks in the mail, she'd beat me to the mailbox and cash those bitches. Now that I was back working and living with Domino for a lil' bit, I had money to myself, and the shit felt good. That's why I had no issue taking Janay shopping.

"I'm paying for all that shit, alright? I ain't never asked you to come out of your pocket, and I won't start today." I dried some of her tears with one hand, while using the other to caress her thigh.

"Okay." She smiled and kissed me on the cheek. "I appreciate you. I haven't had new clothes in forever. Or anything new, for that matter."

"And all that's changing, as of today. You're my woman, and it's my job to take care of you. Shit, you take care of everybody else, so why not?"

She must've liked the sound of that, 'cuz she grabbed my

face and gave me a sloppy ass kiss, making me want to fuck her right there on the spot. It felt good having a woman who not only was supportive, but listened to your feedback and appreciated you, as well.

One hour later...
Man, Janay was too fucking excited to get her ass in Nordstrom's. We'd only been in here for twenty minutes, and she'd gone to the fucking dressing room twice, with over ten outfits. It's cool, though. I liked making her smile and feel good about herself. And with the she was looking in these outfits, I wasn't complaining. Everything she picked out accentuated all her curves. I could hardly keep my hands off of her.

"You like this one, baby?" She twirled out of the dressing room wearing this turquoise off-the-shoulder maxi dress. It was tight, so her ass looked super fat in it. I loved that shit.

"Sure do." I gripped her ass hard, making it jiggle.

"Not right here, Renard." She giggled, trying to move my hands.

"And why the fuck not? You mine, ain't you?"

"Yours, only."

She kissed me, tasting all fruity and shit. My dick hardened, but I knew she probably wouldn't be down for smashing in the fitting room. The store was full of old ass white ladies who would probably call the cops on us. They could never mind their fucking business.

When she was finally done trying on clothes, I took all the outfits she was getting to the front of the store while she went to use the restroom.

"Excuse me sir, but your card has been declined." The cashier was too fucking loud when she said that shit, too. But I knew it had to be a mistake, 'cuz my money was good. Shit, I'd just paid for our meals less than an hour ago.

I shook my head in disbelief. "Nah, run it back."

"I'm not sure if I understand what that means." White bitches, man.

"Try that shit again." I was trying not to yell at her simple ass, but she had me tight. I handed my Visa back to her, and as soon as she ran it, she shook her head.

"What's wrong, baby?" Janay asked, as she walked up to the register. A lil' line was forming behind us too, and it was full of impatient motherfuckers. I didn't give a fuck. They were gon' wait 'til somebody gave me a fucking explanation.

I told Janay to stay in line while I called the bank, and sure enough they told me that my card got reported for fraud a few minutes ago. That shit had Lena's name written all over it.

"Lena, what the fuck did you do?" I barked into the phone when she answered.

I could hear her laughing and smoking a cigarette on the other end. Sounded like she was opening something too. Probably a pack of Twinkies. Lazy, fat ass bitch. "I reported my fucking card stolen, Renard. I don't remember giving you the permission to go get hotel rooms or eat at Red Lobster with my card."

"But it's my card, Lena. I do what the fuck I want to do with my money."

"Not today, bitch!"

I did as my therapist had suggested at our last meeting, and took a deep breath before responding to her. The last thing I wanted to do was let her see me sweat. Plus, if I would've hurt Lena's feelings, she would've without a doubt tried to fuck me over in court. So, I had to play it cool. "Lena, I'm trying to talk calmly and rationally with your ass, girl. That's my account and I'd appreciate it if you left my money alone." It was a damn shame that a grown man had to beg for access to his own fucking money. This lil' stunt she was pulling was nothing but reassurance that I was doing the right thing by leaving her.

She was laughing like a fat hyena in my damn ear. I could almost smell her breath full of Cheetos over the damn phone as she yelled. "Yeah, well my name is on the account too, and since you wanna be buying hoes food and hotel rooms, you no longer have access to that account. Bye, bitch!"

I forgot that she'd listed her name on my account right after we'd gotten married. At first, it sounded like a good idea, since by nature, women were better at managing money than us niggas were. That was my fault, for not taking her off. Thankfully, I had a separate account, too. It wasn't much money in it, but I wasn't about to deny Janay of this stuff, so I used that card to pay for her clothes. Lena was making my life hard, and I wasn't even with her stupid ass anymore.

A few hours later...
The lil' meet and greet with my mom and Janay went pretty damn good. Janay ended up wearing the turquoise dress, and my mom must've loved it 'cuz she complimented Janay a hundred fucking times while we were at her crib. I was happy she liked her, though. I planned on making Janay my wife one day. Just had to get rid of the one I had, first.

I'd just dropped Janay off and was now walking in my lawyer's office. Lena had been served with the papers, which probably contributed to that fuck shit she'd pulled earlier. Now, we were just waiting on her to sign. Something told me this shit wasn't going to go as smoothly as I hoped, so when my lawyer sighed and put his hand on his temple, I knew I was right.

"So, we've run into a small issue. Have a seat, Renard." My lawyer, this white guy named Sam, was supposedly the best divorce attorney in Columbia. Hearing him say he had bad news made me uneasy, though. It made me wonder just how dirty Lena was trying to play.

"What's up, Sam? What is it? Don't beat around the bush, either, man. Let me know something."

"Well, Lena's lawyer reached out, saying that she wanted both alimony and child support. She's claiming that you cheated on her and has shown telephone records proving it.

Child support is due for both children until they're eighteen, but she's asking that it continues until they're twenty-one. And she's claiming that you bring in over three-thousand a month, so she wants two."

"Two what?" He better be saying the words "hundred" or just "dollars", because that's all she was going to get from me. I don't see how somebody could be so fucking money hungry.

Sam checked his paperwork again before answering. "Sorry to say, but two-thousand, Renard."

Yep, Lena was out of her rabbit ass mind. I expected her to pull the child support card, but alimony? She was bugging. "I barely make enough to support myself, Sam." I was lying. Domino paid me a hefty amount as the manager of The Black Palace, but he nor Lena had to know that. Shit, I don't know where she was getting the three stacks a month from, but she wasn't on point. I made more than that, but I still wasn't giving her ass two-thousand dollars per month. She must've bumped that big head of hers.

"Well, did you cheat on her? If so, there's a very good chance that she'll get her way."

"She cheated on me first! I don't even know if those damn kids are mine!"

Sam scribbled some shit down on his legal pad then ran his hand across his bald ass head. Like most old white men, he had a bald spot in the middle of his head, but it was surrounded by hair. I didn't understand that ugly shit. "Well, let's get a DNA test. And if the twins aren't yours, we have proof that she cheated, and no alimony is due."

"Now that's what the fuck I'm talking about." I smiled, and shook his hand. I never imagined I'd be saying this, but if the kids weren't mine, it wouldn't kill me. I just wanted to be done with Lena forever, so I could move the fuck on with my life. She'd taken so much of my energy, time, and money already, that I couldn't imagine having to pay her another penny for the rest of my life.

Later that night...
Walking into The Black Palace, hand in hand with Janay felt good as fuck, 'cuz she was the baddest one in the club; fuck those strippers. The pink dress she was wearing looked so good on her, I doubted we were gon' be here for long. I normally didn't approve of the super short shit for my woman, but my dick damn sure liked it.

Dom and Bailee were in the VIP area, waiting on us, along with Celine and some big brolic dude.

"What's up, y'all?" I dapped up Dom first, and he handed me the blunt, but I declined it.

"Didn't I tell yo' ass to close your eyes around my girl, nigga?"

"Man, get the fuck out of here." I laughed, moving on to giving Bailee a hug. Dom swore up and down that somebody wanted her ass; she was bad as hell, but Bailee was too much like Domino for me. Those crazy motherfuckers belonged together.

I hugged Celine and she introduced me to her dude, Eric.

After dapping him up, I took a seat across from the other couples, and pulled Janay on to my lap. For a while, the six of us just sat around, talking shit, and vibing to the music. Then, the girls took a fucking field trip to the restroom, leaving just the guys. Shit was awkward, because Celine was supposed to be Davion's girl.

Leave it to Dom to break the fucking ice. "You know Celine was my brother's bitch, first. How you met her?"

Eric poured himself another glass of the Ace of Spades that was on the table and laughed. "It was fate, man. I met her through my sister; they're neighbors. Your brother – he the crazy one?"

"Hell yeah." I laughed, watching the strippers walk past with their buckets full of money.

I thought Dom would've gone upside the nigga's head for coming at Davion, but he laughed too. "I don't know what the fuck that nigga got going on. That's my brother, but that nigga is always on some bullshit. I don't give a fuck who Celine's fucking – you, your pops, Davion, or herself. Just don't bring no drama, and we fucking good. I shoot niggas for fun."

"Noted." Eric lifted his glass and threw back his drink, just as the girls walked back to our area.

When Janay got situated on my lap, I felt my phone vibrate. It was nobody but Lena. She called me four times back to back, but I kept ignoring her.

"I don't know why you're ignoring your bitch's calls, man.

She probably wants you to bring her fat ass a Debbie Cake or something." Domino laughed, finishing his blunt.

"That ain't my girl, man. You know I'm getting divorced. Fuck her. And if the paternity test proves the kids ain't mine, I'll never have to talk to her again." Just hearing that sounded so good, although I didn't know how I'd feel if my chaps weren't biologically mine.

"They aren't yours, man. I always wondered how the fuck something so big come out your small ass ball sack."

Everybody except Janay laughed at Dom's retarded ass. Even I had to chuckle a lil' bit, 'cuz he had a point. Jayden and Kayden definitely had their mother's genetic makeup. "We'll see, man."

Just then, my phone vibrated again; it was Lena sending a text, telling me how much she missed me. I let Janay do the honors of deleting it out my phone, and putting my shit on silent, so we could enjoy the rest of our night.

Chapter Nine
DAVION "BABY D" BLACK
The next day...

I'd just left a speaking engagement at Polo Road Park, for the lil' young niggas in the community. I told them the same shit my pops always told me; keep your head up and don't let these crackers tell you what you can't do. They seemed to take in what I was saying, and it was crazy because I'd actually gone in there without being high. It was almost two o'clock in the afternoon, and I haven't touched a blunt, molly, or anything all day.

I guess I was getting the high I needed from Camia. She was really cute as fuck and since she was always laughing and shit, I couldn't help but reciprocate when I was around her. Camiyah wasn't stressing me the fuck out either, and my team was still undefeated because of me. Life was good, which was why I was a lil' confused as to why I'd gotten a call from the coach telling me to meet with him. I was finally doing the right shit, yet these niggas always found a way to fuck with me. Swear to God, people hated to see niggas winning.

"What's up, coach?" I greeted him, as I walked into the locker room.

"I'm going to make this short and sweet, Davion. Have a seat."

"If it's short and sweet, the last thing I need is a motherfucking seat. A seat means this shit is gon' take long." I preferred to stand, just in case I needed to beat his ass.

Coach nodded his head and shrugged his shoulders. "You're off the team, Davion. For more than one reason. Reason number one – you have a woman and a baby staying in your goddamn dorm room, which is unacceptable. Reason number two – we took a sample of your urine without you knowing, and it came back positive. You can't represent the University of South Carolina with this constant behavior. Reason number three – a video surfaced of you and Coach Starkes' daughter – "

"I beat that motherfucking case, nigga!" I barked, getting in the coach's face. He had me fucked up.

Standing chest to chest with me, he got in my face like he was gon' try some shit. "You might've beat the fucking case, but the fact that it's floating around the internet is a bad look for the University of South Carolina! You think you're a fucking man, but you're nothing but a pussy ass little boy!"

Wham!

I wasn't gon' take too much more of him disrespecting me, so I knocked him the fuck out before he had another chance to speak. Blood seeped from his lips, so I reached over the desk and began choking the motherfucker. I wanted him dead!

I felt a pair of hands pulling me off the coach, and I turned around to see that it was the defense coach.

"Get off of him, Davion! That's enough!" He yelled, pulling me off this pussy ass bitch.

"I'm cool. I'm cool."

He loosened his grip on me and pushed me out the door. I couldn't believe this stupid shit, man. Just when I was doing good, they come fucking up my vibe. Instead of driving to my dorm to tell Camiyah about this bullshit, I drove right to this lil' corner store where some niggas I knew were selling some shit. After paying for my weed and molly, I got back in my whip, and received a phone call from Jay.

"Just checking in. How much longer before you bring Domino to me?"

Since Camiyah said Bailee wasn't too thrilled about the double date thing, which was part of my plan, I had been contemplating just saying 'fuck it'. But with all this bullshit going on, I needed money and drugs more than ever, 'cuz being on the straight and narrow was getting me nowhere. And no one seemed to give a fuck about me, either. "I'm working on it, man. I'll have him to you by next week."

"Perfect."

Jay hung up the phone and I rolled my blunt, letting the high take over me.

. . .

Later that night...

Since some nosey motherfucker snitched about Camia and Camiyah living with me, I decided to just pack our shit up and go to my parents' house. I didn't need any more bullshit than I'd encountered today, plus since I was now off the team, there was no need for me to stay in that small motherfucking room. The only person living at the house was corny ass Dedrick, so there was more than enough space for the three of us. And if Camiyah didn't want to be there, she could go to her mama's roach-infested crib, for all I cared.

As we rode in silence, the only thing on my mind was my plan to get Dom to Jay. If she could get Bailee to agree to a double date with us, I was gon' make sure both she and Dom got fucked up. Then, I was planning to put my brother in my whip, and take him to see Jay. Not sure what Jay wanted with him, and at this point, I really didn't give a fuck. I just needed my shit. Shit, famous motherfuckers sacrificed their families for the Illuminati; I see no difference.

Then, I thought about a plan for Shanay. That bitch had released another video today, and people had been hitting me on social media, calling me a pedophile, Lil' R. Kelly, Michael Jackson Jr....all that shit. I was none of that, and had I known her pussy was so young, I never would've fucked. I needed her to lose this motherfucking baby, since the damage she was doing was making me lose the only shit I cared about – my spot on the team.

"You checked on a ticket for me?" I asked Camiyah, as I slowed down at a red light.

"It's $344 round trip. What do you need to go to California for, anyway?"

I almost back-handed her for questioning me, but I decided to let her live. For now. "None of your fucking business. You bought it?"

"I don't have the money, Davion."

I knew she was fucking lying. That fucking dumb ass baby had diapers, clothes, wipes, toys…all that shit didn't come free, so she had to have some money from somewhere. Typical bitch, though. Always lying, and never wanting to give up any bread.

Before the light turned green, I reached over and choked the fuck out of her neck. "Listen to what the fuck I'm saying, Camiyah. I need you to do two fucking things, that's it!"

Her face was turning red as I continued to squeeze the fuck out of her neck. The only reason I let her go is 'cuz I wanted her to be fully motherfucking alert when I said what I had to say. "You listening?"

She nodded her head slowly as tears fell from her eyes. No need to cry about it now; she wanted me so bad, well this is what the fuck it was. "Get my ticket to California, and make sure Bailee and Dom agree to that double date shit, alright? I need that nigga to agree, 'cuz I got some shit to talk to him about. It's important."

"What's in California?"

Goddamn! She was such a nosey ass bitch. If Anna Mae

Bullock was anything like this, I see why Ike rocked her jaw every night. Bitches just wouldn't stop 'til you hurt their asses.

Shit, that was the reason I needed this ticket so bad; so I could fuck Shanay up. Of course, I couldn't tell Camiyah that 'cuz that bitch seemed like the type to fold on a nigga if shit hit the roof. Plus, just having her know my every move wasn't cool. That's not how I moved. I did what the fuck I wanted, when the fuck I wanted. I never answered to anyone. "None of your motherfucking business."

"You're not the same person I fell in love with." She sighed and rolled her eyes.

Love? That shit was comical. "I don't even really like your ass, let alone love you. So let's not act like this shit is more than it is." I was looking her dead in her eyes, so she could get this shit through her thick ass scull. "I will never fucking be with you, alright? Camiyah, you knew just what the fuck this was, so stop playing the victim, alright bitch? We fucked, you lied about being on birth control, and you got pregnant, trying to trap a nigga. You know I'm headed to the NFL, and yo' hungry ass wants a meal ticket, since you ain't never had shit. Just know if you do what the fuck I say I'll cut you a piece of the pie."

She folded her arms across her chest and removed her phone from her raggedy ass purse. Everything about this bitch was raggedy, and it made my dick itch just thinking about the fact that I had a baby with her. "You're not going to the NFL, according to this, Davion."

"Let me see this shit." I snatched her phone and broke that motherfucker in half.

"What the fuck, Baby D? You're gonna get me a new phone!"

"Nah, but if you do what the fuck I told you to do, I won't do that same shit to your face."

I don't know who the fuck she thought she was, showing me that dumb shit. ESPN and the local news were having a fucking field day, at my expense, and for her to throw that shit in my face was disrespectful. And people wonder why I couldn't fuck with her ass. Her elevator didn't go to the top floor.

"It's not that I was trying to pick on you, Davion. I just...I want what's best for you. For us. I need you to – "

"And I need you to shut the fuck up." I interrupted her, as I pulled up at the house. "Get that baby out, and make sure her whining ass goes to sleep. I'm not trying to hear the bullshit tonight. I'll get the bags."

My patience was running low with all this shit going on in my life. I needed to kill that bitch Shanay, get back on the football team, and get Dom to Jay. I could see, smell, and feel the suitcase Jay presented to me along with the fat ass check he promised to write me. Those three things were my main concern; that other shit Camiyah was talking about was null and void.

. . .

The next morning...

The smell of something stank and rotted woke me up. When I opened my eyes, I saw Camia's saggy diaper in my face, so I knew she'd dropped a bomb that her mom needed to get rid of right the fuck now. I didn't know how the fuck a little baby barely weighing twenty pounds could smell so bad. I thought someone had died in my damn room. Shit was foul. I almost fought her ass for funking up my spot like that, then I realized she was just a baby and couldn't control it, but she was gon' have to learn pretty damn quickly.

"Camiyah, change this fucking kid, man." I sat up in bed, looking around the room for her, but she wasn't there.

The shower wasn't running, but I did notice a handwritten note on the dresser.

Davion,
I need some time to clear my head. You have a lot going on right now, and I'm not sure if I can handle both motherhood and you. I need a break. You've hurt me emotionally and physically, and I just need time to process everything. Please take good care of Camia.
See You Soon,
Camiyah

I had to read the motherfucker four times to actually comprehend it. Did this bitch really just leave me with a baby? What the hell am I supposed to do?

Chapter Ten

DEDRICK BLACK

Well, I decided not to kill myself. I guess that's obvious, huh? The only thing that stopped me was seeing my parents' faces when I closed my eyes. I'd been taught at a young age that anyone who committed suicide was going to hell. I didn't want to go to hell, because I wanted to hug my mom and dad again, and I truly believed they were in heaven.

I still didn't feel like I had much to live for, and each day seemed harder than the previous. But, I was getting my mojo back. *Wait, did I ever have mojo? Or is the proper word 'swag'?*

Either way, I was starting to feel like my old self again. And I really mean my old self. I wanted my old clothes, hairstyle, and glasses back. I longed to play in some formula and create medicines, heat, break down rocks, and play with any and all science products. Anybody who didn't like it could just fill their mouths with my sweaty, hairy balls, because I vowed to never let anyone change me again.

Looking down at my phone, I saw a text from Brittany. Although it was hard to ignore it, I did, just as I'd done the others. The text stated that we needed to talk, but there was honestly nothing to talk about. I had things to do.

The first thing on my to-do list for today was rescue the baby in Davion's room. Hearing him cursing and yelling at his sweet baby was way too much for my ears and heart, so I decided to go in there and get her. It was my first time meeting my niece, and she was beyond beautiful. She made my heart flutter the moment I grabbed her from my brother.

"Thanks, man. I can't do this shit right now. I'm stressed."

"I know." I replied, placing my niece on my shoulder. I grabbed her diaper bag from Baby D and told him we were going out for a while, so he could get some me-time in.

I knew Davion had been going through a lot, with those videos leaking and getting kicked off the team, so I had no problem taking my niece off his hands for a bit. Plus, with the way she was smiling up at me, she was actually brightening my mood. I had no idea how people could harm innocent babies – this one was just too adorable for me to even get frustrated with. I had no doubt I'd make a good father one day. That is, if I ever found a woman who loved me for me...

After changing Camia's dirty diaper, I fed her some oatmeal and got her dressed. I took a quick shower while she napped, then brushed my teeth and threw on the first thing I found in my closet. I needed to get out of this house, so my mind wouldn't generate thoughts of Brittany. So, me and Camia were going to take a trip to the mall. All those cool clothes I'd gotten...they're going back. I changed who I was for Brittany, and she didn't appreciate it, so the real Dedrick Black was about to stand up. *Don't call it a comeback!*

I liked my suspenders, my loafers, and my button-down shirts, so I was going to return the clothes I'd gotten and get more of what I was comfortable in. *JC Penney, here we come!*

When Camia and I pulled up at the mall, I couldn't figure out how to set her stroller up. I was a smart guy, but this was one gadget I could not figure out.

"You need some help?" A pretty, thin, caramel colored woman walked up to me and extended her hand. "My daughter has the same stroller. I know how to open it."

She took it from me and opened it without any hesitation, and then grabbed Camia and buckled her in. "Your daughter's adorable."

"This is my...my niece, actually. I don't have a daughter, because if I did, she'd be with me, instead of my niece...or maybe they'd both be with me."

Relax, Dedrick. I had a habit of talking way too much about nothing when I got nervous...

"I get it." She laughed, once again extending her hand, but this time, waiting on me to shake it. Taking her hand in mine, she introduced herself to me after I gave her a gentle handshake. "I'm Venice, like the city in Italy."

"I'm Dedrick. Like Derrick, but with a "d" like the "d" in dog. D...d....Nice to...nice to meet you. Are you from Venice,

Venice?" I knew I was making a fool of myself, but I couldn't help it. Venice was so gosh darn perfect. I was trying to stay focused on her pretty face, but her plump breasts were quite noticeable as they bounced when she laughed. I could have sworn they were screaming at me to free them, and I wished I could have. Her shape was on the same level as Brittany's; her measurements were those of a brick house. *People still said that, right?*

"It's nice to meet you too, Dedrick. And, no." She chuckled, showing off her amazing set of dimples. "That's where my parents met. Neither of them are Italian, though. They were both on a business trip and I guess it was love at first sight. I like your shirt, by the way." Her eyes shied away from me, probably so I wouldn't see her blushing. I was blushing too.

I couldn't believe she'd complimented my attire. I was wearing one of my 'dork shirts' as my brothers would call them, with a pair of my high-waist pants and my Sketchers. *Call me ranch, 'cuz I be dressing.* "Thank you. I'm headed in here to get more, actually."

"Do you mind if I walk with you?"

"Not at all. I'll have to warn you. I don't like girls right now."

She raised her eyebrow and backed up. "Oh, I'm sorry. Are you homosexual? I'd hate to think I was barking up the wrong tree."

I chuckled, which prompted her to do so, too. "Oh, absolutely not! Let me rephrase. I'm just getting out of something that hurt me very much, and in order to keep my heart intact

I've sworn off women for a while." After the night that I almost shot myself, I decided that if women were going to drive me to those drastic measures, I was better without them. Just me and my Chem from now on. Chemicals, that is, not a girl named Kim...

"I totally understand, Dedrick. I never said I was looking for anything serious. Maybe I just need a friend, too."

"Pinky promise?" I held out my pinky finger, and while she giggled softly, Venice wrapped her pinky finger around mine.

"Yes. Pinky promise."

We made our way inside the mall. I pushed Camia and walked beside Venice, and the first person I laid eyes on happened to be Brittany. She was walking out, while we were walking in, and immediately stepped out in front of us.

"Dedrick, please. Can you come back to me? I'm sorry. I'll explain everything. Can we talk? You've been ignoring all my messages."

"Funny you should mention that. You ignored me the entire time I was chasing you."

Aha! She got the hush-mouth, now!

Venice looked away like she was nervous, and shoppers around us stopped to look at the show. Now I see why Domino was rude to most women. They treated you bad, then acted like they were the victims. But, I was tired of being a doormat, and Brittany was about to get a whiff of the karma I was serving.

Brittany opened her mouth to respond, but I placed my hand on her lips to let her know I wasn't interested. "I don't need you to explain anything, Brittany. The only thing I want you to do is get away from me." I surprised myself with my sharp tone, but I wasn't stopping anytime soon. She wanted it, she could have it. "Go stalk whoever gave you that black eye. You should've wanted me when you had me. Now, get the fuck out of my way. Sorry ass bitch! I should've listened to my brother when he said you were nothing but a hoe. You used me, but look who's having the last laugh. Bye, Felicia!"

I took Venice's hand and the three of us walked right past Brittany. "Move, trick! Get out the way!" I sang, referencing a song by Ludacris I'd recently heard. The timing just seemed so appropriate.

When we were a few feet away from Brittany, I looked back and stuck my tongue out at her, leaving her standing there looking stupid. She had no problem with making me look and feel stupid in the past, so I had no pity for her. I would rather use my energy to get to know Venice.

That night...
Venice and I had spent all day together after meeting at the mall. The only time apart we had was when she went to go pick up her daughter, Sarai, from daycare. Now, we were back at my house, and the babies were playing together on the floor, while we sat on the couch waiting for our movie to start. I'd learned that she was a single mother to two-year-old Sarai, who worked as an accountant. She was one

year older than me, but since I was taller, she looked younger than I did. Not only that, but she had a baby face, too.

"I'm really enjoying our time together, Dedrick. It's crazy that we just met today, but instantly clicked. As *friends,* of course."

She made me feel bad, with the latter part of her comment. I went into this thinking I couldn't handle anything else concerning women, but Venice was showing me that not all of them were the same. She was much different than Brittany – she actually wanted me in her presence, and made me feel comfortable being here. *Score!*

Nodding my head and smiling, I admired her beauty. It had only been a few hours, but I felt like I'd known Venice forever. "You're right. You walked into my life at the perfect time, too. I don't know how Sarai's dad let you get away."

"That's mighty flirtatious to say to a friend, Dedrick." We chuckled in unison before she continued speaking. "He didn't really have a choice, though." She shifted in her seat uncomfortably. "He's in prison. And he'll be there for a long, long, time. Not only that, but I found out he'd cheated on me, too. Everything came out once he got arrested. Everything happens for a reason, I guess."

Prison?

I'd seen too many movies where the ex-convict came looking for his woman's new love interest, and I didn't want to be a victim. Venice was beautiful, nice, smart....all that. But, she wasn't worth me losing my life. The information she'd just divulged to me did nothing but secure her spot in the FriendZone.

Noticing the look on my face, Venice laughed and held my hand in hers. "Trust me, Dedrick. He's on major lockdown, and I have no idea when he'd be eligible to even get out. He went to jail for murder."

I felt my heart rate speed up as beads of sweat fell down my forehead. I was so conflicted. I didn't want to, but I liked this girl. Given her situation, I had to find a way to get rid of her, fast. I wasn't a fighter, so I definitely wasn't a killer. At this rate, I should've just stuck with Brittany; she seemed to have less baggage. The problem was, I was so attracted to Venice – it was instant, like a magnet. I couldn't find it in my heart to break hers and tell her we shouldn't see each other, but the last thing I wanted to do was end up on the ten o'clock news. To whoever has the voodoo doll on my love life, you can stop now...

Chapter Eleven
BAILEE RODGERS

The doorbell rang, interrupting this bomb head I was receiving from my man. My legs were reaching my head, and he ran his tongue across my clit in a fast pace, making me squirt all over his face.

After lapping up all my juices, Dom decided to throw some pants on and get the door, since the doorbell had gone off again. Whoever it was, was pretty persistent at ten o'clock at night.

"What the fuck you doing here?" I heard him bark, so I threw on my robe and walked out to the front of the house. If it was one of his lil' groupies or ex hoes, they were going to die tonight. Domino too. Because I'm crazy as hell, I grabbed the baseball bat out the linen closet before running to the door.

"Camiyah? What's going on?" She hadn't texted or called

me to let me know she was coming over, and it wasn't like her to just pop up. Not this late, at least. Since it was her instead of some crazy bitch like Sapphire or Tierra, I put the bat down. "What's wrong, Camiyah?"

Instead of answering, she was just crying her eyes out, but I wasn't sure why. I knew it probably had something to do with that psycho she called a boyfriend, though. And she'd better say something quick, before my psycho boyfriend threw her out of our house.

"I ain't got time for this shit. Bailee, lock the door when she leaves. Then come back in the room and get this dick. Camiyah, don't stay too fucking long."

I chuckled, because I knew he wasn't going to be sitting around, watching her cry, or even trying to figure out why. Dom cared about nobody's feelings but mine.

"Hurry up." Dom kissed me passionately, sucking on my bottom lip as he palmed my ass. "Don't take too long with this hoe, or I'll have to beat my dick. I really want it in your pussy hole, though."

I rolled my eyes and whispered, "I won't." When Domino went back to our room, I grabbed her by the hand and led her into the kitchen where I poured us each a glass of wine. Handing her the Moscato and tissue, I told her to spill the beans.

"It's nothing. Well, it's everything." She sniffled, blowing her nose and then wiping her eyes. I handed her another piece of tissue, because that was nasty as hell. "Thank you."

"You're welcome. Now talk. I'm here to listen, but you've

gotta give me something to listen to." And my kitty was still purring from Domino's kiss, so I wanted her to make it quick.

"It's Davion."

Why am I not surprised? "What did he do, Camiyah?"

"He got kicked off the football team, and I just don't know how he's going to take care of me and Camia now. He also put his hands on me, and broke my phone. Sorry I couldn't call first."

She showed me her neck, which looked slightly swollen and red.

"Did he choke you?"

"Yes." She sobbed uncontrollably. "I just want him to be a better person, Bailee. I want what's best for him."

Sipping my Moscato, I swallowed hard before speaking. I wanted to make sure I was saying this as nicely as possible, because she was vulnerable as hell. I didn't want to be mean, but she had to get it through her goddamn skull. "Camiyah. Baby. You can't change a man, okay? You've done all you could do for him, and now it's all up to him to change. If he doesn't, fuck him. But he shouldn't be choking you or breaking your shit. He clearly has anger issues, and he needs a therapist or a punching bag, not a girlfriend."

I laughed to myself, because Domino had done the same shit to me before. Not choked me, but broke my phone. Those Black brothers were clearly off their rockers, but Davion was a completely different breed. His ass needed to be treated just how he treated others.

"I'm learning that now, Bailee. I'm just…I'm not as strong as you. I need someone to love me."

"Bitch, you have a daughter. She loves you. Your parents might not be shit, but you have a family with Camia. Where is she, by the way?"

"I left her with Davion."

I couldn't have heard her correctly.

"What the fuck did you just say?" I was starting to wonder if she was dropped on her head as a baby. "You left your small, fragile, innocent baby with the same man who just choked you?"

"It wasn't today. It was the other night. I went to my mom's house because I needed to clear my head, and I just haven't gone back to get her yet."

That didn't make it any better.

It took everything in me not to knock some damn sense into her. All I could do was shake my head and sigh. "I wouldn't leave Davion with my doll baby, let alone my real one. Are you crazy?" I would hate it if something happened to Camia, but that was Camiyah's child, not mine. And if she wanted to put her daughter in the line of fire, so be it. Better her than me.

She looked embarrassed as she shrugged her shoulders. "Can I just stay here? Just for one night? I'll be gone in the morning before you wake up. I just need a good night's sleep. My mom kicked me out because she thought her boyfriend was gonna flirt with me."

Her mom was trash for that, but I also felt like Camiyah

was trash for leaving Camia with Davion. But, someone could say the same about me, since I aborted my child. So I guess it was best not to judge, even though it was hard to justify Camiyah's actions. "Sure. One night, though. Domino doesn't like a lot of traffic in his house."

I walked her to the guest bedroom she'd be sleeping in and handed her a towel, wash rag, and toothbrush from the linen closet. "And do me favor, Camiyah. Boss the fuck up, and take care of your daughter. You don't need to depend on a man for shit. For nothing."

That was rule number one of being a woman. Domino could leave me today, and although I'd be missing the hell out of him, I wouldn't miss no money or no meals.

"I understand. Thank you, Bailee."

When I got back into the room with Dom, he looked mad as shit. Too bad I was about to piss him off even more. "I let her stay for the night, but I told her she had to go tomorrow."

"You know I don't like all these motherfuckers in my house, baby. Shit, I'm trying to get Weezy out, but he's so scared Lena's gon' find his bitch ass."

I chuckled although I knew I shouldn't have. I didn't think the domestic violence was funny, it's just that Dom made even the worst situations seem comical.

I climbed in bed to give him a massage, then sat on his dick, riding him long and good enough to release all the stress he had built up…

. . .

The next day...

Ever since I'd won the showcase, my phone has been ringing off the hook. Private messages, friend requests...a lot of females trying to book appointments with me and a lot of niggas trying to shoot their shot. It was a known fact I was Domino Black's girl, and he was known to shoot niggas for less, so all the flirtatious messages and offers really took me by surprise. Especially all these messages from Tony Marshall. The nigga just wouldn't quit.

"This nigga must want me to kill him." Domino laughed, as I showed him the messages Tony Marshall had written me. I told him three times that I belonged to Domino, but the nigga was acting like he was fucking retarded and couldn't understand. Hell, I thought it was apparent the night Dom shot up his album release party when he was looking for me.

"You have nothing to worry about, baby. I'm all yours. I'm too crazy for another nigga. Nobody wants me but you."

Dom palmed my ass and fed me his tongue in a powerful, magnetic, spine-tingling kiss. We were out in broad daylight, but my man didn't care. He was one of the few hood niggas I knew who didn't mind PDA, and I soaked it up as much as possible.

"If this bitch is another minute late, she's canceled. Time is money." Dom hissed, as he broke our kiss. I knew he had a conference call set for three o'clock that he needed to prepare for, and it was already almost one thirty. The realtor was supposed to meet us at one o'clock.

I wanted the five thousand I won from the showcase to go toward the down payment to my shop, but Domino wasn't having that. He told me to either save it, or spend it on myself, because he was planning to handle everything. I won't lie, letting a man have that much control over my future scared the hell out of me, but thankfully, I have a man who sticks to his word. The nigga was full of surprises. He'd met with a realtor without my knowledge, and had decided on the building we were currently standing in front of. It used to be a shop ran by a lady named Lucille, but she passed a few years ago, and it'd been vacant since. I couldn't wait to go inside. Domino was particular as hell, so I knew if he had given his consent, the place wasn't bad at all.

"Sorry I'm late. There was an accident on I-26. I'm Kelsey. You must be Ms. Rodgers." We shook hands, but I caught the bitch looking at Domino like she wanted a piece of his chocolate. If she kept trying me, she was going to get more than she bargained for.

"Yes, I'm Bailee. I'm sure my *boyfriend* Domino told you all about what I'm looking for. Hopefully this is it."

"It is."

Kelsey opened the door to the salon and when she turned on the light, I instantly fell in love. It wasn't the biggest salon, but it was perfect for what I wanted. There were three shampoo bowls in the back, five stylist stations, and even a room in the back where I could get someone to do eyebrows or nails. There were two single restrooms – one for employees and the other for the clients. Altogether, it was about four thousand square feet, and I loved every inch of it.

Without even having to ask me, Domino must've known I wanted it, because he went ahead and asked Kelsey how much he needed to write the check for. While they talked about all the logistics, I walked around the shop, envisioning my clients coming in and out of here, leaving with smiles on their faces and their hair laid. I planned to hire only the best stylists in Columbia to work alongside me, and with the power of social media, I had no doubt that it wouldn't take long for me to find them.

A few hours later...

Domino had gone to work out, so I decided to take the time to clean the entire house. I wanted to cook him a nice, hearty dinner too, so after scrubbing the house from top to bottom, I changed into a tube dress and went to the grocery store.

You ever felt like there was someone following you? In the produce section, I felt a strong presence behind me as I reached for the cabbage. Someone grabbed my hand, causing me to scream.

"Bailee? Calm down. I wasn't trying to scare you."

I turned around to see Jason standing there, flashing his pearly whites at me. I didn't see anything to be smiling about, though. His weird ass had scared the shit out of me. "If you weren't trying to scare me, then what the hell were you trying to do? Why are you following me, Jason?"

"Don't flatter yourself, Bailee. I'm not stalking you or anything. I saw you and just wanted to say hi." Jason hesitated, looking around as if he was waiting on either me or someone else to say something. Breaking the awkward silence, he finally spoke up. "How are you doing? I called you a couple of times, but when I asked Celine about you, she said you'd gotten back with your ex. Are y'all okay?"

I hated when guys did this. There was no need for him to try to pry, because his corny ass was just a distraction. And he didn't even succeed at that.

Before I could answer, a nice looking white guy walked up behind Jason, pushing a cart and clearing his throat. "Jason. Are you, uh, ready?" He sounded irritated and anxious, and Jason looked nervous with him being here.

"Sorry, Bailee. I'll...I'll talk to you later. Oh and you...you don't have to mention to Celine or Eric that you saw me, alright? I appreciate it." He walked away as quickly as he'd come over here, and I swear I saw the white guy pull him by the waist.

I think my predictions about him being gay were true. Men like him killed me, because their dishonesty was often what put my fellow African-American sisters in harm's way when it came to AIDS. Jason wasn't my issue; I just hoped he would one day walk in his truth. His little secret was safe with me, though.

Once I got back home and started cooking, the doorbell

rang. When I opened it, there was a delivery guy standing there, holding a beautiful bouquet of flowers. "Are you Bailee?"

"I am." I nodded my head and took the flowers from him. "Are these for me?"

"They aren't for me." He laughed, handing me the card that went with them.

As soon as I read it, I was chasing him down the driveway. "Sir, I can't accept these. Please keep them."

"But, I was told to deliver them to you, Miss Bailee."

"Well look in the phone book, and find another Bailee to send them to. They can't come in this house, and don't deliver me anything else from him. You got it?" I handed him the bouquet and ripped up the note in his palm. "Now please get out of here, before my man comes back home and kills you."

I waited outside until he drove off, and when he did, I ran back in the house and wrote Tony a message on Instagram, telling him to never in his life deliver anything to me again. I didn't even know how he knew where I was living, but I guess when you're a celebrity, you can find things out. He'd better stop while he was ahead, though, because Dom's crazy ass was nothing to play with.

Later that night...

Tony hadn't responded to my message, so I took that as him agreeing to leave me the hell alone. I deleted the message I'd sent to him out of my phone, just as I saw Domino's headlights pulling into the driveway. I quickly put my phone back in my apron, and pulled the pan of pork chops out of the oven, as his key turned the lock. Despite the fact that we'd been living together for a while now, I still got anxious anytime he came home. My heart pounded, I got butterflies in my stomach…all of that, as if it was the first time I was seeing him. I guess that's what being in love does to you.

I ran toward the door before he could even get all the way inside, ready to hug and kiss all over my man. He'd been gone from me all day, and I'd missed the hell out of him.

As we hugged, he palmed my ass roughly. "I know yo' ass ain't go out the house in this short ass shit, Bailee. I thought you valued your life."

My dress wasn't that short.

"All I did was run to the grocery store, baby."

"Ain't it niggas at the grocery store? Let me know if you found a grocery store just for bitches only. And not none of them nigga bitches that look like Lil' Boosie, either."

I could not stand this nigga.

He brushed my lips with his and pulled me closer to him. "I love yo' ass girl. And if I catch a nigga even breathing in your direction, I have to dead him. You wearing this shit out when I ain't with you don't make it no better. This is a "fuck me" dress. Only wear it when you're with me, 'cuz that's the only time you're getting fucked."

Blushing, I rolled my eyes and playfully hit his broad, strong chest.

"I'm dead fucking serious, Bai. I put it on yo' future grave."

"*My* future grave?"

"Yeah, 'cuz if I catch a nigga looking at you, both of y'all getting murked. Him first, though. 'Cuz I'ma fuck you good one last time, and I don't need him watching."

Stupid.

"You must not know how fucking fine you are." Dom kissed me, making my heart race, my pussy pulsate, and my nipples harden. His kisses and touches were so orgasmic. "You know you're beautiful, right?"

I always blushed so hard when he complimented me. While I'd never been one of those girl who lacked self-esteem, I never was cocky, either. I knew I was beautiful, but having a man like Dom who reminded me every single day just how sexy I was, made me feel like the most beautiful woman in the world. His love was raw, because that's just who he was, but I wouldn't trade it for anything in the world.

Standing on my tip-toes, I gave him a nasty, sloppy kiss on the lips. "I love you, Domino Black. And I promise not to wear this dress again, unless it's just for you."

"Good. 'Cuz I can see your pussy print and your ass cheeks, so I know them lame ass motherfuckers in the streets can. And I'd hate to have half the niggas in Columbia walking around with no fucking eyes."

"Boy, you're crazy." I chuckled as his lips roamed from mine to my ears neck. My love tunnel was pulsating, anticipating the pipe he was about to lay on me. Since he was wearing tight workout clothes, his erect dick was even more obvious.

"Bend over." Domino bent me over before I could take his orders. When I was bent over, touching my toes, my dress rose and my man immediately slid his dick inside, filling me up. Stroking me deeply at a rapid pace, Dom pulled my hair as I threw my ass back. The sounds of our skin slapping together echoed throughout the house, and within seconds, we were cumming together. Feeling his warm seeds settle inside of me felt so good; I never wanted this man to let me go.

Chapter Twelve
DAVION "BABY D" BLACK

I still couldn't believe Camiyah had left me with that fucking baby, but it was all good. She was probably trying to teach me a lesson or some shit, and as much as I hated to admit it, it was working. I think she wanted me to stop taking her for granted. It wasn't that I'd been meaning to, it's just…I don't know. I like her, but at the same time I don't, 'cuz she swear she knew what was best for a nigga. I wish she'd just let me be.

Anyway, my goofy ass brother Dedrick was helping me out with the baby a bit, but I was actually enjoying her lil' cute ass. She was finally growing hair and shit, so she was looking like a girl instead of a boy cabbage patch doll.

As far as everything else in my life…man, this shit was difficult. Not being on the team hurt like a motherfucker. Them pussy niggas lost their game last night; had I been on the team, the outcome would've been different. NFL recruiters were at all the games, and now that I was no longer apart of the team, my chances of going to the NFL were growing slim. That's why I was currently waiting on Coach Cannon to get his bitch ass to his car, so I could talk some sense into the nigga. Yep, I was in the parking garage, waiting by his whip, with Camia's lil' body strapped across my chest in a lil' sling thing that Camiyah left. She was sleeping so peacefully, I hated to wake her ass up with the commotion that was about to go down.

When I saw the coach's pussy ass walking toward his car, I bent down a little and pulled out my pistol. Drastic times called for drastic measures.

"What are you doing here, Davion? You're not supposed to be here!" Coach Cannon yelled when I pressed the gun up to his head. One of his hands was on the handle of his car, and the other was trying to block the gun, but I had a pretty good grip on his forehead. "Please don't kill me!"

"You weren't supposed to be here either, motherfucker. Your ugly ass mama should've swallowed. And why shouldn't I kill you, motherfucker? You killed my football career!"

"I didn't! I'm sorry. I'll do anything you want. Just please... I have...I have a family."

Was he serious? Did he not see the fucking baby strapped to me?

"Nigga, I got a motherfuckin' family, too! And you didn't give a fuck about kicking them out my dorm or putting me off the team, did you? How the fuck I'ma feed my kid in the future if I can't go to the NFL?"

Tears streamed down the bitch ass nigga's face, which made me laugh hard as hell. To be such a large sized man, he was really a pussy. And, he was dumb as fuck, because I wasn't about to kill nobody in a fucking public garage. Just had to shake some fear in him.

"What is it, Davion? You're trying to get back on the team?"

Shoving the gun harder on his temple, I laughed. "Nah, bitch. I'm trying to be the waterboy. Of course I'm trying to get back on the fucking team!"

"I'll talk to the other coaches and let you know…I promise."

"You got 'til tomorrow. Or that precious family of yours will be turned into ashes." I meant that shit. I wasn't going to kill him right now, but that didn't mean I wouldn't fuck with that man's family. Fuck them.

I took the gun from his forehead, then shot in the air so he'd know I was serious. I strapped Camia back in her car seat and rolled out, anxiously awaiting the good news I'd be getting tomorrow.

The next day…

It was no surprise that I got a call from the coach today, saying I was back on the team, if I wanted to be. The nigga they'd replaced me with was trash as fuck, so in my opinion, it shouldn't have even taken me fucking with Coach Cannon. But, the important thing was that I was back on.

I called Camiyah to give her the good news and to tell her to come get her baby so I could go to practice, but the dumb bitch didn't answer the phone. Dedrick was home, so he said he'd watch her for me. After changing her wet diaper, I fed her and left her with my brother and the lil' bitch he'd been bringing around. Her name was Italy or some shit. Paris. France. Malaysia. Some fucking place I ain't never been.

On the way to practice, I decided to roll up a blunt and lace it with molly, just to get in my groove. Being high felt so fucking good that if I wasn't high, I didn't feel like I could function. And I needed to be able to function without any type of issues today, since I hadn't been to a practice in a while.

Just as I pulled up at the practice field, Jay's number popped up on my screen. This nigga was really bugging me, because it felt like he hit me up to check the progress of everything on the daily. I didn't know why he wanted Domino so bad, but my curiosity was starting to get the best of me.

"Jay. Why the fuck you want my brother so bad, man?" I asked, after ensuring him for what seemed like the fiftieth time, that everything would work out.

"Your brother owes me." His tone was low, dry, and sharp as a knife. "And if I don't get it from him, I'll get it from you."

No the fuck he wouldn't.

"Wait a fucking minute, man. That's not what we discussed." I never agreed to pay back Dom's debts; hell, I didn't even know there were debts. "Plus, that shit don't add up. You claim he owes you money, but you're willing to pay me to bring him to you? Ain't that losing money, partner?"

Laughing, Jay replied, "I never said he owed me money. Your brother owes me everything he has, and if I don't get it from him, I'm coming for you." Before I could ask another question, I was introduced to his dial tone, and I was too scared to call back. Jay had fucked my mind all the way up, so before I got out the car, I smoked another blunt, just to ease it. I popped a pill, too. Anything to make me function instead of having to deal with the bullshit life was handing me, was alright with me.

After practice...
Usually, when I had some shit I needed to get off my chest, I went to my partner Weezy. He was usually easy as fuck to talk to, and would give me the brotherly advice I needed if I couldn't get it from Dom. We'd smoke a lil' bit, drink a lil' bit, and I'd walk away feeling a lot calmer about whatever the fuck was going on. But lately, he's been unavailable anytime I needed to talk to his ass. He didn't even want to get high with me anymore, which was crazy, since he was the one who turned me onto drugs healing my pain. I knew Dom had put his ass as the manager of The Black Palace so he had responsibilities, but damn, he could at least make time for his lil' bro. A nigga was out here getting kicked in the balls by life, with no one to turn to.

I decided to roll up on my boy at The Black Palace, just because I figured he'd be here. I was right. I spotted his run down Honda the minute I pulled into the lot. That shit was as beat up as he looked after Lena whooped his ass. He once told me that he drove it, which was the same car he'd had since eleven years ago when he turned sixteen, because Lena wouldn't let him get a new one. She thought a new car would attract new bitches. Now that he was supposedly off that bitch, he needed to get himself a new ride, 'cuz that shit was one mile away from turning the fuck off and never turning on again.

"Weezy! What's good my boy? Long time no see." I dapped him up after spotting him talking to some of the bartenders. Although he was hesitant for a few seconds, he reciprocated.

"I been chilling, man. Working. Getting my shit together. And spending time with the finest woman Columbia has got to offer."

"Oh, well I know you ain't back with your wife, then." We chuckled in unison as we sat down at the bar. I asked the sexy bartender to pour me a shot of gin, and then I chased it with a shot of Hennessey.

"You better be careful, man. You're not even old enough to be drinking. So please don't get drunk, man."

I laughed so hard at that shit, because this warning was coming from a nigga who was known to get so drunk that he didn't know his own name.

Ignoring him, I waved the bartender down for another

drink. "I'll take some Dusse." I handed her my shot glass, and when she returned it filled to the brim, I threw it back. "Another."

"No. He's good, Sofia." Weezy said to the bartender, trying to be my fucking daddy or some shit.

I stood up and bossed up to his bitch ass. I wasn't good until I said I was good, and I needed another fucking drink. "Nah, fuck him, Sofia." I handed her the same shot glass I'd been drinking out of. "I need some Patron, and I need you to give it to me now."

"You're mixing white and brown, man. That ain't good. Take a break."

"The only thing I'm breaking is your neck, motherfucker." I swung at him, but missed, so he grabbed my arm and twisted it back. "Fuck you, Weezy! That's why your new bitch is gon' leave when she sees how much of a pussy you are! You're Lena's bitch. You probably suck her dick, too!"

Wham!

My jaw stung after feeling his fist go across my face. He knew I was right, though. "Too bad you don't have the balls to do that to Lena, pussy! I hope she fucks you up 'til the point of no return. Fuck you, Lena, your new bitch, and your ugly ass kids."

"Watch who the fuck you're talking to, motherfucker! Your fucking mouth is gon' get you fucked up! That's the same reason Celine don't want your ass!"

"Fuck you just said to me, player?" I got in his face, ready to fuck him up. He didn't know a motherfucking thing about me and Celine, and I felt disrespected as fuck. And how the fuck did he know she didn't want me, anyway?

I guess Weezy thought he was a boss, 'cuz his lil' stumpy ass wasn't backing down from me. The nigga should've had those same balls when it came to that big-foot bitch he called a wife. "Yeah, nigga, I said it. Celine was just here, and she wasn't with you. You're too fucking disrespectful, man. You gotta grow up."

Wham!

I wasted no time hitting his ass back. "Nigga, you can suck my dick! You, your new bitch, your old bitch…all of y'all!"

"Get the fuck out, Davion. You need help, man!" He pushed me out the door hard as hell, and I got in my whip and drove the fuck off. That nigga Weezy had changed; I didn't know who had him thinking he could fucking talk to me like that, but that nigga was now on my hit list.

The next day…

The shit Weezy said last night about Celine not being into me anymore really had a nigga fucked up. I mean, did I want the bitch? Nah. Well, I don't know. Maybe. But whether I wanted her or not, she wasn't allowed to step foot into The Black Palace with another nigga. Motherfuckers must've forgotten that I still owned a portion of the club. The last thing I was gon' do was be disrespected in my own place of business, which was why Weezy's days were numbered. And if what he said was true, Celine's were too.

Right after I left practice, I decided to go pay that Spanish bitch a visit, to see what the fuck her stupid ass had going on. And if she fucking lied to me, I was going to smack her dead in her round ass face. I'd been leaving her the fuck alone for a while, but now that Weezy dropped a bomb on me, I had to remind that bitch who she was fucking with. And if Weezy was lying, I wanted to make sure she was still miserable as fuck without me.

"Answer the motherfucking door, Celine!" I roared, knocking hard on her door. I knew she was there, 'cuz her car was outside. There was another car there, too, but I didn't give a fuck if her funky ass friends were there. I wanted to see the bitch, just to show her what she was missing out on.

She still didn't come to the door, so I kicked that shit until I heard footsteps.

"What are you doing here, Davion? Leave now! Salte!"

Did this bitch just call me salty?

"I'll pass on leaving. I'm cool where the fuck I am. Let me in. I got you this." I pulled out a small box of chocolate covered cherries from my pocket. I remembered one night she told me she liked those nasty shits, so I picked her up a box before coming over here. I covered the expiration date on them, because they were old as fuck. No wonder they were ninety percent off.

She took the box from me, but still didn't let me in her crib. "Gracias. Now go!"

That shit had me hot. Celine was a damn fool if she thought I was gon' let her treat me like some sucker.

"Bitch, you think you're gonna just take something I bought you and kick me out? You got another thing coming." I was ready to slap the Spanish out of her.

"Davion, it's not a good time."

As she was trying to close the door, some burly ass nigga walked up behind her. "Do we have a problem here?"

This nigga was acting like he wanted smoke, but he must not have known I was with the shits too. "My problem is that you're at my bitch's crib. Who the fuck are you, partner? Is this the nigga you were at the club with, Celine? You ain't tell him you were my woman?"

"Davion, I am not your woman! Leave! Te odio!"

"I don't know who the fuck Teddy O. is, but I'm about to beat you back to Spanish Harlem, Maria Maria!" I yanked her by her hair, as she tried to push my body out the door.

Before she could fully push me out, the dude threw a punch that landed right in my mouth. I charged at him, but he swung again. The only reason he was getting off on me is 'cuz I'd snorted some lines right before I pulled up. He was pretty strong, so I wasn't gon' fuck with him today, but I was coming back to beat both of them up later, once I was no longer high.

"This ain't over, motherfuckers!" I yelled, walking back to my car. Celine and whoever that Hercules motherfucker she had over there really had ya boy fucked up. Before leaving her driveway, I rolled a blunt and sprinkled some coke on my weed. The only thing that made me happy was doing this shit; I'd never stop.

Chapter Thirteen
CELINE GOMEZ
A few days later...

I didn't want to get out of Eric's car, but I knew I needed to get to class. Eric had surprised me at school and taken me to San Jose, and now that I was back in time for my last class of the day, I wasn't feeling it. I didn't want to do anything without mi novio. I just wanted to be wrapped in his strong arms. *El era tan perfecto.* Oh, and I forgot to add that during our little lunch break, we had amazing sex in his backseat, which was the main reason I was feeling so sluggish an hour later. He had definitely given it to me good; my body was still numb. Muy Bien...

"You're dragging your feet, but you better get out the car, before I carry your ass to psychology class. Make me proud, baby." Eric kissed the top of my forehead.

"I'll try." I reciprocated his kiss, but on the lips. He had the best lips. I think the best part about them was that they were used to encourage me. *Alentar.* Not to disrespect me, like Davion did. I still couldn't believe he'd come to my place acting muy loco and demanding to know who I was at the club with, but I was happy Eric put him in his place. Davion deserved everything Eric gave him, plus more.

I climbed out of Eric's car, after making him promise I would see him later.

"You'll see me after you do the lil' shit with your homegirls. I ain't trying to be around all that gossip and shit. I want you all to myself."

"I want you all to myself, too, papi. You know I'm muy celoso." It's true, I was jealous and possessive as hell, when it came to him. I didn't want to let him leave my side for one second, but he was right – I needed my time with my girls to unwind.

"You got me all to yourself," Eric promised. "Nobody's taking your sexy ass away, you just gotta be sure this is what you want."

He was.

Not only was he mature, sexy, and could make my pussy throb at the sight of him, but I loved how direct he was. He was a real man, and he didn't have a hard time telling or showing me that I was who he wanted. El era muy vocal, and I appreciated that. Girls liked to know how men felt about them sometime.

Blowing him a kiss, I watched my man drive off. I couldn't wait to be back in his presence in just a few hours.

. . .

Two hours later...

After the craziness that had gone down with Davion and Eric the other day, it felt good to just relax. And that's just what the hell I was doing. Janay, Bailee, and I were having a much-needed girls' day. I'd been so wrapped up with my new chulo, Eric, and Janay and Bailee had been booed up too. So it was nice to have some time with mi amigas. After class, Janay and I met up with Bailee at the nail shop, and we were currently sitting in the pedicure chairs, drinking mimosas.

"I really like Eric for you, Celine. Be glad you dodged that bullet named Davion. He's getting worse, girl. Out of fucking control."

I nodded my head, responding to Bailee. She'd told me how he was supposedly trying to make it work with the mother of his little nina, but then put his hands on her. I didn't tell her about the instance in the library where he almost raped me, but he was definitely not a good person. I tried my hardest to see the good in people, but in Davion, I couldn't find any. Everything about him literally made me want to vomit. I couldn't even look at a football, thanks to him.

Eric, on the other hand, was everything a girl like me could ask for. Es un sueño hecho realidad. He was really the man of my dreams. "I like him for me too. He's muy guapo, patient, funny, and just...everything Davion wasn't." I chuckled to myself thinking about the other day, when Eric gave Davion two well-deserved blows to the face. There was no doubt about the fact that Eric would protect me anytime he felt the need to. He literally was all I'd wanted in a man, and I was so blessed to have found him. I guess the prince really does come after kissing a frog.

"And everything he'll never be." Bailee quipped, interrupting me from my thoughts. We chuckled in unison and nodded our heads, agreeing that Eric was ten times the man Davion was. Bailee then turned to Janay, who was sitting on the other side of her, quiet as hell. That wasn't like her. "What's wrong? Why are you so quiet?"

"No reason. It's just crazy how we're all in a good place right now."

She was right about that. At one point, I was so stressed about Davion that I'd started losing weight in all the wrong areas, and having migraines every day. Now, ask me how often I was stressed. Nunca. Eric did everything in his power to make sure I was happy, and I appreciated him for that. He was almost too good to be true.

One hour later...

When my chicas and I walked outside of the nail salon, I couldn't believe my eyes. "Aye Dios Mios!" I yelled and cried, at the sight of my car.

This was the second time some shit had happened to my car, and this had Davion's name written all over it. I didn't know who else would want to slit my tires and bust a window.

The brick that was used to bust my window was actually sitting the backseat of my car. I couldn't believe we hadn't heard the commotion from inside, but I guess the culprit was quick about it. My car, though? Por que? Davion really had some fucking nerve...

"Who the fuck would do this?" Janay asked, inspecting my car as I dialed a tow truck. Next would be my insurance company, and at this point, I knew they were sick of me.

Bailee and I looked at each other, both knowing the answer to Janay's question. Era obvio. It was pretty obvious to me. Davion just wouldn't let me live in peace, and it wasn't only annoying, but scary too. I now felt like I had to watch my back at every turn, and until he got over me, I'd probably be living in fear.

Later that day...

"If you're not fucking the nigga, then why would he do some shit like that, Celine? It was bad enough that he'd come over here the other night."

Eric was pissing me off, acting like I had something to do with what Davion did to my car. I didn't, though. Some people were just sick in the head, and he was one of them.

The moment the tow truck got my car to a shop, I called Eric to let him know what had happened. He picked me up from the shop, and even paid for the repairs to be done, but he wouldn't stop insinuating that I was messing with Davion. Era absurdo.

I glared at him for a good minute before answering, because I'd sang this song with him one hundred times today, already. "Papi, I told you, I have no idea. No se. But I swear, I'm not fucking anybody but you."

"Yeah, well, you need to handle your nigga before getting even more involved with me. I don't play those games, Celine. He's a kid to me and I ain't going to jail for fucking murder. I'm a grown motherfucking man and I'll knock his fucking cap off, football star or not. What's not gon' happen is my life or my girl's being in jeopardy. You can live your life like that, but I'm not; I'd kill his ass first."

Eric pulled out his wallet and peeled out a stack of fifties, then handed them to me. "Take this money, get you an Uber and a hotel room, and stay safe."

An Uber? A hotel room? "Eric, por que? Why can't I stay with you? Why can't you stay here?" By this time, I was crying; my emotions were all over the place. It felt like he was just dumping me out into the ocean to swim alone.

"I told you, baby. This is kid shit. I want no parts. If you were mature, you'd realize that this shit is dangerous, and you'd want to get out of this house, too. Just for a little while."

I was mature, but I wasn't as scared as Eric thought I should have been, I guess. Davion was muy estupido but I didn't understand what going to a hotel *alone* would solve. I needed Eric with me. I didn't know if Davion would try anything else or not, though. He was hard to read.

In my psychology classes, I'd learned about people like Davion. He had a lot of shit going on. He was spoiled, entitled, and an all-around asshole. Now that I was no longer giving into him, he was trying to find ways to make my life miserable.

Eric grabbed the gym bag he'd brought over, and planted a kiss on my forehead. "I'm out, alright? Hit me when you're drama free."

I wanted to scream for him to stay or to come to a hotel with me, but there was no use. He was right. I couldn't fully move on with him or anyone else, until I had all this stuff with Davion straightened out. The last thing I wanted to do was put Eric or my relationship with him in jeopardy.

Chapter Fourteen
DOMINO BLACK
The next day...

While Bailee was in one of the guest bedrooms doing some broad's hair, I decided to get some work done. She was as nosey as a fat ass math teacher on test day, so I could never work from home unless she was sleep or not here. I didn't mind, though. It was cool having my woman under me all the time.

The first email I saw was one from Tierra's stupid ass, sending me a damn picture of an ultrasound. She was dumb as fuck, though, because once I zoomed in, I saw that shit didn't have her name on it, unless her name was Kevia Smith. And I doubted that very fucking seriously. That shit had me hot because she'd been bothering the fuck out of me and now I had proof it was all a lie. One thing I didn't appreciate is motherfuckers annoying me over bullshit, so Tierra was about to get a visit from me. And it wasn't gon' be the type she wanted.

I went in the room to give Bai a kiss and tell her I was out. The minute I got into my whip I hit Tierra's line. I asked her if her mom was home, and since she said no, I told her I was on the way over. I could tell by the excitement in her voice that she thought this shit was about to come out in her favor, but she was lucky if she came out alive. Annoying ass bitch.

"Yo. Open up the fucking door, T!" I kicked her shit in 'cuz she was taking too long. "Yo fucking fat ass ankles broke or something?"

She was just standing there when I walked in, instead of moving those motherfuckers to open the door.

"No! Why? And why the fuck did you kick down my door?"

"'Cuz you were taking too long to open the motherfucker. Fuck is that email about, Tierra?"

Rubbing her fake ass pregnant belly, she smiled. "Our baby, Domino. She's growing so big. Doesn't it make you wanna be a family?"

Before I could answer, her ugly ass poodle ran in the den and jumped on my leg, trying to fucking hump it or some shit. Horny ass dog. He had the wrong one today. Tierra was telling him to stop, but I took matters into my own hands. I just grabbed the motherfucker by the neck, and tossed him out the window. Her apartment was on the third floor, so that ugly shit went flying off the balcony, landing on its back. The lil' fucker would've survived, had a car not sped by at that exact moment. He was whimpering 'til he couldn't whimper no more, but I didn't give a damn. Hoped he enjoyed Doggy Hell.

Crying, Tierra threw her hands up in the air. "Domino! Did you just kill my mama's dog?"

"Is an orange orange, bitch? Sending me fucking fake ultrasounds and shit. Leave me the fuck alone, Tierra, alright? Next time, it's gon' be you out the window, just like that ugly ass dog."

I stormed out, leaving her crying on the floor, but she was lucky she still had breath in her fucking body. I was so close to kicking that imaginary baby out of her damn stomach.

As soon as I got in my car, a call from Kelsey, the realtor I'd been working with for Bailee's shop came through my phone. "This is Domino. What's up?"

"Domino. It's Kelsey. I need you to meet me at the shop please."

I hung up and headed toward the shop I'd planned to buy for Bailee. Kelsey sounded like something was wrong, but she'd better hoped that nothing fell through with the shop, 'cuz I was on her ass if it did. Most of the money had already been paid, and if something went wrong on her end, she was gon' pay me all my bread back plus interest.

"Thanks for meeting me here, Domino. I wanted to let you know that I'm not sure that I can continue working on getting this building for you."

"And why the fuck not? I gave you over half the money." I didn't play about my funds, and every motherfucker from here to Mexico knew it. "Cat got your fucking tongue? Speak the fuck up, 'cuz I don't have all night." She was staring at me with her mouth open, like she was fucking retarded, and I hated to have my time wasted. "Bitch, are you slow? I asked you a fucking question. Either answer that shit, or get back on the slow bus that you rode in on."

Smirking, she shook her head and tucked a string of hair behind her ear. "I got this message from Bailee earlier." She handed me her phone, showing me an Instagram private message from Bai's account. I laughed like fuck when I read the message, 'cuz my bitch was real life crazy.

"I don't see the problem." The message didn't say much, it just told her she appreciated her finding the shop for us, but to keep her eyes to herself. And from the way Kelsey was staring at me right now, licking those ashy ass lips of hers, I could see why Bai felt like she should give her a warning. Bailee was really the female version of me. She didn't play no fucking games with these bitches. She had nothing to worry about, though. I wouldn't fuck with Kelsey if there was a gun to my head telling me to. I would just have to die that day.

"I didn't like the way she came at me, Domino. I mean, you think I'm a good realtor, right? I did my job well...right?" Kelsey walked toward me, then tried to brush my arm. I could tell she hadn't used lotion in a few days. Either that, or she had a serious case of eczema. I wanted no parts, either way. I couldn't understand bitches with long bundles and dry ass hands. She had her priorities fucked up.

"Bitch, if you don't get that snake skin off me." I removed

her hand from my arm, and she folded her scaly hands across her chest like she had an attitude or something. I should be the one with an attitude, 'cuz now I had to sanitize my whole damn arm.

"I've never worked with someone I've been attracted to, Domino. It's hard to watch you and Bailee...it's hard to watch you do all this for her. The moment I met you, I wished it was me you were doing all this for instead."

"So does every bitch in Columbia. If it's hard to watch, then close your motherfucking eyes when she's around. Now you just keep doing your fucking job as the realtor, and I won't say shit to Bai about this, alright? And you might not know it, but that's saving your fucking life." Bailee had fucked me up before, so I had no doubt she'd really hurt this scrawny bitch standing before me.

"Fine. I'll try to keep it professional."

"Don't try. Better get like Nike and just do it." I pulled out my checkbook from my wallet and handed her the check I'd written.

"What's this for?" She asked, as she accepted it. After reading it, her face turned red. "For Cetaphil?"

"Yes." I nodded my head as I put my wallet back in my pocket. "Go take care of that skin. Please. If your hands are that dry, I can only imagine your pussy. Shit probably feels like the Sahara Desert."

She rolled her eyes and walked away, hopefully taking her ass to Walmart for that damn lotion.

. . .

Later that day...

I wasn't the type to stick my nose in grown motherfuckers' business, but Bailee had been begging me to talk to Baby D about both Camiyah and Celine. I really couldn't give a fuck less about what the nigga was doing, 'cuz I'd given up on him a long time ago. But, as a favor to my bitch, I decided to try to talk to his knuckle-headed ass one last time. He was definitely on some bullshit, from what both she and Weezy told me. Even Dedrick said he was wilding, and that nigga usually kept his opinions to himself.

I was surprised that when I told that nigga to come by The Black Palace, he didn't question me. Usually, he had a response for everything, hard-headed ass.

"Sit down, Baby D."

"Nah. I prefer to stand." He folded his arms across his chest and looked down at his feet. He was probably doing that so I wouldn't see how red his eyes were, but I'd already peeped that shit.

"D. I don't know what the fuck you got going on, but I need you to calm the fuck down, alright? You can't be fucking up people's cars 'cuz you're mad they ain't giving you no pussy, bruh. Nor can you be wilding on your baby mama. After all, man, she's taking care of your fucking seed. Do you even do your part with Camia?"

I already knew Dedrick and his new bitch had Camia most of the time, but I wanted my pussy ass brother to admit he was a deadbeat.

"I have Camia more than you have your kid! You ain't gon' never have one, since your bitch likes to abort!"

Wham!

I smacked the fuck out of him, causing him to drop to the floor. "You watch what the fuck you say to me, motherfucker!" Davion really had lost his fucking mind, talking to me like I wouldn't shoot his ass. Baby brother or not, I would fuck a nigga up for speaking on that shit, or speaking ill about my girl.

"Fuck you, Dom! You think 'cuz you own this shit, you're so tough! Fuck you and The Black Palace!"

That nigga got worked up for no fucking reason. I don't know if it's the guilt, the drugs, or if he was just plain retarded, but he had a fucking problem. Laughing at his rage, I lit a cigar and puffed smoke in his face. "I am the shit, nigga. And that's because unlike your punk ass, I work for mine. Everything in this motherfucker, I own. I ain't no pussy ass bitch like you, who feels like the world owes me something. I eat niggas like you for breakfast, and the only reason I haven't fucked you up yet is 'cuz you're my brother. But your time is winding down, motherfucker." I stood up and got in his face. "I will beat you into bad health if you ever come out your fucking mouth about that abortion again, nigga. Actually, don't even mention my bitch. Shit, don't even say the word "baby" around me, nigga. You feel me?"

"Nah. I don't feel you. You gon' feel me, though. Watch yo' back, motherfucker."

I didn't have to watch shit. Not a nigga or bitch on this earth put fear in my heart.

Once Davion left my office, I turned on my computer and saw I had an email from Tatianna. Just as I hit delete on that motherfucker, one of the dancers ran into my office. Those hoes knew they were supposed to knock first, but the only reason I didn't curse her simple ass out was because she was crying and all frantic and shit, so I knew something was wrong. If those bitches were fighting again, I was taking all their earnings for a week.

"Fuck wrong with you, running up in here like you've lost the lil' bit of mind you got?"

She looked like she'd just seen a ghost. "Domino! Your brother! He…he just got hit by an 18-wheeler outside! Hurry!"

I followed her out, and for sure, Davion's car was smashed in on the driver's side. I dialed 9-1-1 and ran to my brother's side, reliving the night our parents died damn near the same way. He was barely breathing, so I tried to perform CPR in hopes of saving his life. There was blood everywhere, and I could tell he wasn't conscious at all. I just hoped he could hold the fuck on 'til the ambulance came.

Chapter Fifteen
WEEZY
At that same time...

The shit that went down between Baby D and me at the club had left a sour ass taste in my mouth, man. Maybe it was because I was changing for the better, and I just wanted him to be on that same wave. I felt partially responsible for his behavior, since I was the one who'd introduced him to drugs as a coping mechanism, and I regretted that shit. Thanks to his brother, I was now living a better life, and I had a bad feeling that Baby D wouldn't get to if he didn't stop snorting that shit.

But, I'd have to talk to him about all that at another time. Maybe once both of us cooled the fuck off, 'cuz a lot was said, and although the shit was just words, words could hurt.

I didn't have time to be worrying about what the fuck he had going on right now. I had my own shit to deal with. I was back at my lawyer's office, twiddling my thumbs like the nervous fucking wreck I was. The results of the DNA test I'd taken were back, and Sam was about to open them. The results would change my life, and my pockets forever, and I was hoping for the best.

"I've got some good news, and I've got some bad news." Sam sang, after opening the envelope.

I was sweating fucking bullets, and didn't have time for his games. White people loved to fucking play when it was time to be serious. "Spit it out, man. What that shit say?"

"You're the father of Jayden, but not Kayden."

What?

"Yo' how the fuck that happen? They're fucking twins, man. Popped out the same big coochie two minutes apart. Born May 5, 20 – ". There had to be a mistake.

"I know their birthdays." He laughed, handing me the results. Sure enough, this nigga was right. That shit said my paternity was 99.9% for Jay, and 0% for Kay.

"How the fuck is this shit possible?"

"It happens." Sam shrugged his shoulders and opened his bottle of water. "Sometimes, two different sperms can fertilize the same egg. Yours is just a rare case. That does mean that you won't owe Lena any alimony, though, because it's evident she committed adultery. However, you'll be required pay child support for Jayden, since he's yours. And visitation…if you choose to go that route, will be for Jayden, only. I mean, if you two want to work something out for Kayden, you can. But, it's not required."

This shit was crazy, man. It's like I had to fucking forget

Kay existed. How the fuck was I supposed to explain to my lil' girl that she was the product of her mama being a hoe?

Breaking my thoughts, Sam continued. "We can go ahead and get the child support papers for Jayden together. Might as well put yourself on it, since she's asking for it. It's a lot less painful that way, and to the judge, you look responsible."

That wasn't what I really wanted to do, but seemed like I didn't have a fucking choice. I didn't want shit deducted out my paycheck, 'cuz I didn't think my salary was the government's or Lena's business. Once your name was in that system, the government had access to all your shit, and that's why I hated child support. Don't get me wrong, I did for my kids, and would continue to, but I didn't need shit being taken out of my check before I even got a chance to see the motherfucker.

I thanked him for his time, but my mind was still fucking blown. I decided to pay Lena a little visit. I needed answers, and now that I knew at least one of them was mine, I wanted to see my kid.

Pulling up at the crib I used to share with them was bittersweet. So many bad memories still lurked there, but I did miss having a family. Even though it was a fucked up one. Going home to Dom and Bailee every night wasn't the move, but I did like that I had a peace of mind.

"Daddy!" Jayden and Kayden yelled, running toward me as I walked through the door. The twins were already tall as fuck like their mama, but now they looked like they'd grown another foot since the last time I saw them.

I hugged each of them separately, then together. I squeezed Jay a little harder, though. I guess because I knew he was mine, but his sister wasn't. That wouldn't make me love her any less though. I'd raised her. I just had to find a way to break the news to them, when the time was right. They weren't old enough to understand the shit yet. Shit, my ass was damn near 30-years-old, and I barely understood it. My head was all fucked up.

"I love y'all, man. I missed y'all." I kissed the top of each of their big ass heads. I didn't realize how much I loved their asses 'til recently, when I had to take a DNA test. The drugs were probably clouding a lot of my judgement, but since Dom made me stop doing them, I'd been able to face my realities head on. It's crazy how an addiction could make you neglect the ones you were supposed to love most. That's why I wanted that nigga Davion to get it together. His lil' one deserved better, just like mine did.

"Are you taking us out somewhere? If so, can we go play ball?" Jayden asked, grabbing his basketball from the corner of the kitchen. Lena had done some remodeling in here; it looked nice for once. Updated.

"I can. We can go wherever y'all wanna go. Go tell your mama bye. We won't be out too long, though, 'cuz I need to come back and talk to your mama about something."

"You can come tell their mother hello, Renard. Walking in my goddamn house without speaking. You ain't got no motherfucking manners."

This bitch had twins by two different motherfuckers, yet she wanted to talk to me about manners? Word.

But that was a conversation for later. Not one that the kids should be around for, so I kept quiet. "Hello to you too, Lena." I walked in the den and couldn't believe my eyes. Lena looked about eighty pounds lighter. I could actually see her neck and it looked like she was able to tie her shoes. For once, she didn't have a damn Debbie Cake hanging from her mouth, either. She looked like the Lena I met and fell in love with. "You look...different."

"And you still look like shit."

She might've looked better, but that attitude was still terrible. "You know what, fuck you, Lena. I'll have the kids back later."

"When the kids come back, I need to talk to you. It's important."

That was funny, 'cuz I needed to talk to her too. "We can talk, 'cuz I need to talk to yo' ass, too. But just know I'm not coming back to be with you, Lena."

I didn't want her to have it misconstrued in her head. I was here to see the kids and to tell her what I'd learned. Nothing more, nothing less.

"I'm dying, Weezy. And I need to make sure you're able to handle the kids on your own, okay?" The softness in her voice told me she was serious. I knew when people had illnesses like cancer, they lost a lot of weight, so I was wondering what was going on with her.

"What you mean you're dying? Fuck is going on?"

"We'll talk when you drop the kids off, alright? Just get them loud fucking kids out of my presence so I can rest."

I chucked her the deuces and went back in the kitchen to get Jayden and Kayden for the day, with my mind wondering what the hell I was going to hear when I brought them back.

Later that night...

Holding Lena in my arms as she cried, I shed a few tears myself. She told me she'd been diagnosed with Sarcoidosis, and the fucked up thing was that she knew it before I even left. While she was beating my ass, she knew she had this terminal disease. And instead of taking care of herself, she continued to eat all the wrong shit, and smoke like it was nothing, which didn't help with her lungs.

According to what she'd told me, the doctors weren't sure how much longer she had to live, but this shit definitely had a possibility of taking her out. And there was nothing they could do to stop it.

"I just need to make sure the kids are taken care of, Renard. I need you to step up. I've been having appointment after appointment and they've been going with me, but I'm tired of them seeing me like this. I want them to enjoy the rest of their adolescence, not take care of me."

No wonder she hadn't been bothering me as much as she could have, aside from that credit card shit. She was sick.

"I'll move back in, Lena. I'll be here to help you. And them."

"Thank you, Weezy."

I leaned down and kissed her on the forehead, feeling bad about all the evil thoughts I'd had about her and all the times I wished she'd die just so I wouldn't get beat. Yeah, she was wrong for putting her hands on me, but I felt bad as hell for her. I couldn't imagine knowing my life was about to end. I couldn't promise her we'd get back together, but I did promise to be there for her and the kids while all this was going on. I'd missed a ton of appointments and diagnosis, and despite how I felt about her as a person, I couldn't bear to miss any more. My kids — well kid — was on the brink of losing a mom, and that was pain I haven't even endured yet. So, I felt it was only right to be there for them during this time. I just hoped once Janay read the long text I was planning to send to her, she would understand. Hopefully we could pick back up where we're leaving off once everything settles with Lena's health, but right now, I could no longer make her a priority, and although it was the right thing to do, it hurt me to have to do that to her. Damn, man.

Chapter Sixteen
DEDRICK BLACK
At that same time...

*B*rittany wouldn't leave me the heck alone, so I agreed to let her come over since she claimed she wanted to talk. I wanted her to get all of her words out of her heart and off her chest, because after today, I never wanted to hear from her again. I wished you could mute people in real life.

"You've got about ten minutes, Brittany. I'm expecting company soon." I sat on the couch beside her and she immediately pulled me into her lap.

"I want you back, Dedrick. You were the nicest guy I've ever had."

I know. Too bad for her, I wasn't nice to her anymore. I had developed a backbone, and it was as strong as the perfume she was wearing.

"Brittany, go bother the guy who gave you the STD or the

one who gave you the black eye. Was it the same person?" She looked embarrassed. "Actually, I don't care. Just leave."

I stood up from the couch and grabbed her hand to lift her up, but she pushed me back down. That Brittany was a strong one. Who am I kidding? I'm lanky, so it didn't take much for her to move me.

"Sit, Dedrick. I'm sorry I hurt you. Physically and emotionally. The guy you saw at my house that day...he did both things to me. And as badly as I want to get away from him, I can't. He's very controlling."

"He didn't look like he was forcing you to leave with him. You did it willy-nilly, Milly-Vanilly." I folded my arms across my chest as I replayed that scene in my head, remembering how awful she made me feel about myself by dissing me. Why would she try to diss me, when I just wanted to kiss her?

"Dedrick, you don't understand! He's abusive. I'm not safe. I don't want this life anymore."

"What life is that, Brittany? One of a thot?" I'd learned that word from my brothers, and being that it stood for 'that hoe over there', I thought it was quite befitting.

"Dedrick...if you let me explain – "

"Well, I'm not, so, please don't let the door hit ya where the good Lord split ya."

I was on a roll today.

I could tell she was shocked by my words, but I was learning to be cutthroat. The last thing I wanted was to let her hurt me again. She didn't look like she was about to move, so I decided I was going to make her. Taking a page out of

Domino's book, I picked up some of my chemicals from my in-house lab and poured them on her.

"Dedrick! Why would you do that?"

Her white shirt was now purple, blue, and pink, thanks to the harmless fluids I'd splashed on her. *She's gon' learn today!*

"Get out!" I raised my voice slightly. I didn't want to wake Camia up, who was in the other room sleeping.

"Dedrick, I'm a prostitute!"

Did I just hear her correctly?

Gripping her arm, I asked, "What did you just say, Brittany?" Prostitutes walked the streets and waved down cars, begging for men to be their customers. They did God-awful things for a little bit of change. The same freaky things Brittany used to do to me, she was doing with every Tom, Dick, and Harry that rode down the street. This didn't make sense. "Brittany, did you say you're a prostitute?"

Instead of responding to my question, she nodded her head. "It's true. The guy you saw...he's my pimp. I'm trying to leave that lifestyle, but he...he won't let me."

I was baffled. It was a known fact that Brittany's family was full of money, so why would she have to prostitute? Something didn't seem right. I was born at night, but not last night.

"I don't believe you. Actually, I take that back. Whether you are or aren't...it's okay with me. I, Dedrick Black, no longer am in love with you. So, you can go screw your customers and your pimp and leave me the heck alone! I have more fish to fry!"

"What?" Brittany chuckled.

Darnit, I said that wrong. "I mean...there are more fish in the sea! Goodbye, Brittany."

The smile that was on her face a few seconds ago quickly turned into a frown. "Fine, Dedrick. I was willing to open up to you and was hoping you could save me, but I guess not."

"Now you see how I felt about you. Bye, Brittany. Make sure your next victim is clean, though." This little revelation made me appreciate the new woman in my life so much, because Venice would never. I'd definitely dodged a bullet. Well, although I did get hit – well, stung...

The moment I opened the door so Brittany could leave, I saw Venice standing there holding Sarai with a hurt, confused look on her face. Had I not had on my good boxers, I probably would've pissed on myself.

"Venice. It's...it's not –." I reached out for her arm, but she yanked it away from me.

"Save it! You're no different from the rest, Dedrick!" Venice spun on her heel and ran toward her car.

Brittany laughed and whispered in my ear. "You should've just stuck with me."

I gave her a kick in the booty with my KSwiss sneaker and watched her stumble off the porch. I didn't want to be abusive towards her, but she had to go. She'd possibly just messed up the best thing that's ever happened to me.

When I got back in the house, I ran to get my phone, so I could call Venice to explain. But, the fact that Domino had called me eleven times made me put her to the back of my mind for a minute. Calling him back was a priority, because he wasn't the type to call that many times unless something was wrong.

"What's wrong, Domino?" I asked, the moment he answered the phone.

"It's Davion, man." He was crying, and my brother never cried. I didn't even see him crying at our parents' funeral. "He…he got hit by an 18-wheeler. Get to the hospital, man. We're at Baptist."

Before I could ask any questions, he'd hung up. I went in the room to grab Camia and did fifty in a forty-five, because I was trying to get there quickly.

When we got to the hospital, there were reporters all over the lobby. I saw Bailee and Domino sitting in a corner away from all the madness.

"How's he doing? He's not – "

"No. He's not dead." Bailee answered, as she wiped a falling tear from Dom's eye. "But, he's not doing good, either. He's actually in a coma, and they found a lot of drugs in his system. Right now, they're unsure of how much damage was actually done."

She showed me where his room was, and took Camia from me, since babies weren't allowed in ICU. Taking a seat next to his almost lifeless body, I began crying as I reached for his hand.

We'd never been close, but this was my brother. My baby brother. I was supposed to protect him. "I'm sorry, Davion. I'm sorry that I was never the strong protector you needed. I'm sorry we never had much in common, but the one thing we do have in common is our blood. I wish I could've saved you. You needed more help than I could give you, and I'm sorry you're feeling like you're fighting on your own. I promise you one thing. When you get out of here, we're fighting it together. Me, you, and Domino."

"Don't speak for me." Dom entered the room, wearing a scowl on his face. "This is one hard-headed ass nigga, right here. Love the fuck out of him, though. I hate to say this, but everything happens for a reason. Hopefully this will be his wake-up call."

Hopefully. I'd watched my little brother change drastically since the death of our parents, and not in a good way.

"You think he'll ever be able to play football again?"

Domino shook his head. "They said probably not. He probably won't be able to walk again."

Wow. This day just kept getting worse. Football was Davion's dream, and I couldn't imagine his life without it.

For the next two hours, I sat holding my brother's hand. He couldn't hear me. He couldn't see me. He had no idea I was there. But I kept telling him how much I loved him. I prayed to the high heavens to give him more time with us. Taking him from us right now, when he hadn't even reached his full potential yet, was just too unfair.

Chapter Seventeen
BAILEE RODGERS
A few hours later...

Today had been an emotionally draining one. Davion was a complete ass, but you couldn't help but feel sorry for him. I mean, nobody deserved to be in an accident with an 18-wheeler, and put in a coma. I wouldn't wish that on anybody, not even an abusive, rude, male chauvinist like him.

Dom was taking it the hardest, though. He told me they'd argued right before the accident, so a part of him was feeling like it was his fault. He'd been having major mood swings, so as soon as Camiyah got to the hospital, I handed her Camia and decided to leave for a little while. I didn't want to say the wrong thing to Dom and start an argument. Plus, he needed his time alone with his brothers. And I wanted to go home to freshen up.

I decided to call my parents and have them meet me at

the shop after I took a quick shower. It was now officially mine, and I'd started decorating and getting everything ordered, like the chairs I wanted, and the different stands and products I wanted. I was so close to having my cosmetology license that I could taste it, and then instead of going to work for someone, I'd be able to run my own shop, at the age of twenty-one. Crazy, right? Dreams definitely come true, and what Domino had done for me was proof of that.

"This is beautiful." My dad complimented me, walking into the shop. "It's called Bailee's House of Beauty?"

"Yep." I beamed, revealing the sign. It was covered in paper to be put on the front of the door, but I wanted to show it off.

My sister and dad seemed impressed, but all my mom did was walk around nit-picking. "The sinks are small. The floor has a crack in it there. And the paint is chipped right here."

It was just like my mother to find something wrong in *everything* I did. She wasn't stealing my joy, though. Not about this shop. This was what I was most proud of.

"Ignore her. We're proud of you, Bailee." My dad assured me, giving me a hug and a kiss on top of the head.

After showing them around for a few minutes, they left, and I decided to do some tidying up. Anything to take my mind off everything that was going on.

No one knew I was here, so when the doorbell rang, I was confused as hell. Standing outside the door was an older gentleman, wearing a dark gray suit and a black hat. He was carrying a briefcase.

"May I help you?"

I didn't open the door all the way; just enough so we could hear each other.

"Are you Bailee Rodgers?"

"Who wants to know?"

"It's about your boyfriend, so if I were you, I would let you in."

"And what's my boyfriend's name?" I quizzed.

Without missing a beat, he replied, "Domino Black."

I decided to let him in, only because I was curious about what he had to say. "Look, I don't know who the fuck you are, or why you're here, but you'd better make it quick. If you know anything about Domino, you know he doesn't play about me."

"I'll be quick. I just need you to help me with something." He opened the suitcase and there was a ton of money. Like, a ton. More than I'd seen in one lifetime. "Where is Domino?"

"Why?"

Chuckling, he pulled out stacks of money and waved them in my face. "Because if you tell me where he is, all this can be yours. He bought you this place?"

"What's it to you?" I snapped. This man was really irking me, and I wished more than anything that Dom would walk his ass through the door right now, but I didn't tell him where I was going when I left the hospital, so he probably had no idea I was here.

"Domino has chump change compared to me. You understand? You tell me where he is, and I'll make sure you're set for life."

"My man does a good job of that already. No thanks. Get the fuck out of my shop." I whipped my pepper spray out of my back pocket and sprayed it all in his eyes.

"Bitch! You're a crazy ass bitch, just like your man!"

"You'd better believe it!" I sprayed him until he grabbed his suitcase and ran out. Locking the door behind me, I quickly called Dom to tell him about the stupid shit that had just gone down.

One week later...

I hadn't been doing much for the past seven days except going to class, working on the shop, and watching Baby D sleep at the hospital. He was still in his coma. I'd also still been ignoring social media messages from Tony Marshall left and right. After I told that man to never in his life deliver flowers to me, he started asking me to be the leading lady in his next video, as if Domino wouldn't shoot both of us. I told him no, but he wouldn't stop contacting me. He was now bugging the fuck out of me, and if Dom wasn't such a hothead, I would've told him about his antics. Each time I'd block him from one account, he'd make another, and send me a message. I was trying to spare the poor boy's life by handling it myself instead of telling Domino, but he had one more time to send me a disrespectful ass message before I had Dom bust a cap in his ass.

I haven't seen the guy who came to my shop anymore, but I was watching my back everywhere I went. Not only that, but Dom had hired a bodyguard by the name of Kris to follow me everywhere when he couldn't. Dom was super protective over me, and he'd hired Kris to be his eyes and ears. So far, he'd done a good job of it, because I could barely turn around without Kris doing it first to make sure I wasn't in danger. He was huge, too. About six foot eight inches, weighing at least 350, and he never wore a smile.

Kris was with me now, which was slightly embarrassing, considering I was at the local pharmacy skimming through the feminine product aisle. What I was looking for wasn't tampons, though.

"Don't say a word about this to Domino, okay? I want to tell him when I'm sure and on my own time. This is kind of a big deal."

Kris made a cross over his chest and smiled. I made him also pinky swear as I internally debated over which brand of pregnancy test I wanted to buy. The last thing I wanted to get was some cheap, inaccurate shit; I had a feeling I already knew what it was going to say, though.

My cycle was now four days late, and when we had sex for the past week or so, something felt different. My body felt different. I think deep inside, I wanted to be pregnant, because I'd be giving Domino the one thing I took away from him. Even though he claimed he'd forgiven me for it a while ago, I still felt guilty about it. I wanted to make it up to him. And a baby would definitely change his mood around, because he'd been extremely depressed since Davion's accident.

After much deliberation, I finally settled on a ClearBlue digital test, and once Kris and I arrived at home, I couldn't help opening the box and peeing on the stick. It said to use first morning's urine, but I was too anxious. And thankfully, Domino was at the hospital and then would be going straight to The Black Palace; I needed to be alone at a time like this. I had hoped that I was, but if I wasn't, I needed time to heal from the rejection.

Watching the test change from blank to "pregnant 2-3" made my heart flutter. I couldn't believe it! There was really a little person growing inside of me! God had given me another chance, and this time I would do right by my man, my body, and my seed.

Since I'd gotten the hunch that I could be expecting, I had been trying to figure out cute ways to tell Domino. Now that I knew for sure, all that planning was going out the window. I dialed him up to see where he was, and since he was headed to the club, I told him I'd meet him there.

I got there in record time, with Kris trailing behind me.

"Damn, Roadrunner. I just talked to yo' ass five minutes ago." Dom kissed on the lips gently as he opened my car door.

It was really eight minutes ago, though. I got here in eight.

"Domino, baby! Guess what?"

"What? Why the fuck yo' face so red, looking like Rudolph?"

Rubbing my flat stomach, I exclaimed, "I'm pregnant!"

"You fucking with me?"

"No!" I took the test out of my purse and waved the test in his face. "See? It says pregnant!"

"Damn, Bai. I can read!" His face scrunched up. "What the fuck that 2-3 mean? Two to three damn kids? I beat it up *that* good?"

I rolled my eyes and laughed. This nigga was crazy if he thought I was about to birth some damn triplets. "No, silly. That's how far along I am. Two to three weeks pregnant."

Without saying another word, Domino lifted me up and began planting kisses all over my belly. "You bet not abort this one, or I'ma stuff you back in your mama's hairy coochie and abort yo' ass."

Crazy ass.

"I'm not, baby. I'm happy."

I meant that, too. I was at a point in my life that I used to pray to be in. In cosmetology school with a shop, a loving man, and now a baby on the way. Life couldn't get any better.

*L*ater that night...

When Domino came home from the club, he ran me a nice, warm bath and put rose petals all over the bathroom floor.

"You didn't have to do this, Dom."

"Oh, I know. I ain't had to do shit. I'm doing it 'cuz I want to, and 'cuz I definitely want some of that pregnant pussy tonight. That shit gon' be wetter than the ocean."

"Nasty. That's what got us in this position in the first place." I laughed, playfully hitting his arm as he removed my clothes.

"You so fucking sexy, Bai. I know this past week has been crazy, but I never want you to forget that I love yo' ass. And I'll do anything for you, except let you leave me."

I had no intention of leaving, so he had nothing to worry about. "I love you too, baby." I patted my stomach, which of course, was still flat as hell. "*We* love you."

Dom's tongue went from my mouth to my neck, then ran across my nipples, arousing me. It felt so warm against my soft skin. When I felt his lips drop to my lower set, I trembled as his tongue dipped in and out of my opening. I was so moist down below, and with the way his tongue felt brushing across my clit, I knew my release was underway.

"Dommmm! Dommm!" I shouted loudly, as he sucked on my g-spot while caressing my round breasts with his hands.

I buried his head deeper in my middle, and within seconds, a wave of fluids came gushing out from my pussy onto his beard and tongue.

"Oh yeah. You got to stay pregnant. That shit is ten times better." He lapped up my juices, then placed me in the tub to wash me.

"Why do you love me like you do, Dom?"

Sometimes I still couldn't believe that a former player such as himself could want me for the rest of my life. Out of all the options he had, he was as head over heels for me as I was for him. I'd never had a love so strong, electrifying, crazy, or dangerous before, and I loved every minute of it.

"'Cuz you fine as fuck, that pussy stay wet, and you ride like a pro."

He washed my back as I rolled my eyes. "But for real though. I love you with all my fucking heart, girl. After what Sapphire did to me, I didn't think I'd ever want another relationship, but the moment I met yo' cute ass at my club, I knew you were different. Shit, you showed me that shit by not throwing ya panties at me the first night. You could've been a lil' hoe like all these other bitches, but you ain't. You're loyal, and I swear that's all a nigga needs." I laughed, because he was right. Dom was so used to women bowing at his feet, and I didn't do any of that. He continued to lather my back with body wash as he placed a kiss on the nape of my neck. "You stuck with me through all my bullshit, and I appreciate that shit. You rare. And that's exactly why I'm giving you this."

I turned around to see him holding a black velvet box with a huge princess cut diamond ring. He clapped once, and Gerald Levert's "Made to Love You" started played lowly in the background. My heart beat rapidly as tears of joy filled my eyes. The song, the bath, this ring…everything was…perfect.

I took a deep breath before asking, "Domino? Is this – "

"Bailee Rodgers. You've changed the fuck out of me, baby. I don't know what I would do without you, and I damn sure ain't trying to find out. I love yo' ass, and if you ever were to marry another nigga, I'd have to chop your ring finger off. So, you gotta take this ring, and promise to love and fuck me good forever. You with it?"

That was the hoodest proposal ever, but it brought so many tears to my eyes, because I knew it was from his heart. I couldn't even speak; I was too busy crying.

I nodded my head as my fiancée put the ring on my finger. "I love you so much Domino."

"I love yo' ass, too. Now get out the tub, before yo' ass become wrinkly as hell, and I don't want you no more."

We chuckled in unison and once I got out the tub, we made love for the first time ever as an engaged couple. And my man was right – pregnant sex was *much* better.

Chapter Eighteen
DOMINO BLACK
The next day...

Although Davion was still in his coma, I had shit to take care of. A business to run. Well, two businesses. Jerrod told me the crowd at The Black Palace Miami was getting thick, so I suggested we hired some more girls. He was supposed to be the one to do that shit for me, but his punk ass son got the chicken pox so I had to do it. Hell, I ain't even know kids still could catch that shit.

As I was packing for my trip, Bai's nosey ass was scanning my briefcase, probably trying to figure out how long I was staying.

"Why you taking condoms?" She reached in my bag and pulled out a box of Durex condoms. "Why the fuck do you even have condoms, Domino? You damn sure don't use 'em on me."

"And I never fucking will. They ain't for me, baby."

I wasn't lying at all. They were for Weezy's stupid ass, 'cuz he was coming with me. He'd recently gotten back with Lena – or whatever the fuck they were doing. But I knew that nigga couldn't keep his shit in his pants, so I picked up a box of condoms for him. I didn't want to tell Bai's nosey ass, 'cuz of the way he did her lil' friend. He'd completely stopped fucking with her the moment Lena told him she had a terminal illness.

"Liar!" Bailee threw one of her heels at my head, and the shit knocked me in the ear, causing it to bleed. "I'm your fiancée, and I'm pregnant, and you're buying condoms, Domino? Every time you go to Miami, you're fucking around on me, huh?"

"Nah, I'm not. But if you want me to, I will."

Her face went stone cold. "What kind of fucking answer is that?"

"'Cuz you steady blaming me for shit that I ain't doing, Bailee!" Niggas couldn't stand that shit. Bailee should've known me well enough to know that if I wanted to cheat on her ass, I'd do it so well that she'd never find out. Why the fuck would I pull out a box of condoms right in front of her?

Her face was all sad and shit, and although those accusations got on my damn nerves, I didn't want her to be upset or sad. "Come here, baby." I reached out for her fine ass and sat her on my lap. "Those fucking condoms ain't mine, alright? They're for Weezy, in case that nigga fucks up. And why the fuck would I buy Durex? Those are the kind they give you in middle school when you ain't fucking nobody but yourself. You gon' still have babies with those shits. I'm a Trojan man."

I hadn't worn those cheap motherfucking Durex condoms in my life, and wasn't gon' start today. This was the type I knew Weezy used, but Bai should've known I wasn't fucking with these. These shits looked like they'd pop before getting 'em on. Especially given how big my joint was.

Finally, she smiled. "You're right, baby. I'm sorry. I guess it's just the hormones."

"Hormones my motherfucking ass. You crazy as fuck, just like me. That's exactly why you're my bitch. Now let me get some of that good pussy before I leave."

My plane was leaving in three hours, so I had a lil' bit of time.

"First, bend down and apologize to him."

"To who?" Bailee asked with an attitude. Black women and their attitudes, boy...

"My dick. Apologize for blaming him of wearing those toddler ass condoms."

Bailee laughed, but bent down and pulled my throbbing dick out of my pants. "I'm sorry, Prince Charming – "

"Whoa, whoa. Who the fuck is Prince Charming? Call my dick something manlier. Like Big Daddy Long Stroke."

Bailee rolled her eyes and kissed my dick, then took all of me in her mouth slowly. Her mouth was wet and hot, and my dick felt good scraping the back of her throat. I fucked her face 'til I was close to cumming, and then I bent her over and stroked her from the back, and we came simultaneously.

. . .

*L*ater that day...

We'd landed in Miami almost thirty minutes ago, and I was already ready to go the fuck home. The minute we walked into The Black Palace Miami, a crazy odor hit me.

"Y'all got fish on the menu?" I asked this nigga named Pat, who was one of the cooks.

He laughed and shook his head. "No sir boss. Chicken is the only meat."

"Well one of these hoes needs a good douche, 'cuz it smells like flounder and catfish all through this motherfucker."

The club was full of strippers practicing on the stage, and sitting on the couches were the hopefuls. Weezy and I put on social media that we'd be hiring ten more girls on the spot this evening that would have to start tonight. At least fifty showed up, but given the body odors in the vicinity, a whole bunch of hoes would be going home.

We called the wanna-bes up on the stage, in sets of five. The deejay turned on Young Blacsta's "Booty" and they began dancing. Before he got to the chorus on the song, I'd told the deejay to turn the shit off.

"All y'all bitches have two left feet. All five of y'all gotta get the fuck on through."

One of the girls opened her mouth to argue with me, and I swear it smelled like all the odors I'd been smelling stemmed right from her tongue. "You didn't even give us a chance."

"You clearly didn't give a toothbrush and Listerine a chance. Get the fuck out, before I call a dentist on you."

The entire club erupted in laughter, but this was no laughing matter. It should've been against the law to walk around with breath that stank. The shit was explosive.

After calling up a few more groups of five, we'd found our ten and sent everyone else home. Some of them stripper bitches were mad they didn't get a chance to audition, but they'd better scratch their asses and get glad, 'cuz I had the ones I wanted.

A few hours later...

Weezy and I decided to stay at the club for a while, so of course we popped open a bottle of Ace of Spades while we chilled in VIP.

"What's going on with you and Lena, man? Why you went back to that bitch? You like getting fucked up by Godzilla?" I was just curious as to how he'd gone from Lena to Janay, back to Lena. Especially after finding out Kayden wasn't his. I didn't know a nigga alive who would happily go back to a house where he got his ass beat. Fuck kind of shit was that?

"I gotta be there for her, man. She's dying. She needs me. Those kids need me."

"Nigga, we all gon' die one fucking day." I finished my drink, while he sat there looking like a kid who just lost his damn best friend. "Perk up, motherfucker. I get that you wanna be there for the kids, but when you gon' do what the fuck you need to do for yourself? That's why she was always able to take advantage of your ass. You don't show her you have a backbone. Shit, *do* you have a backbone, nigga?" This nigga was as soft as a pillow, and it killed me. I couldn't even be mad at Lena for fucking the nigga up; he was the one letting her do it all these years.

"And what the fuck you call what you're doing with Davion? You're at the hospital damn near every day; aren't you babying that nigga?"

Laughing, I poured myself another drink. "No comparison, my man. That's my brother. He didn't beat my ass, take my manhood away, cheat on me, and he damn sure didn't punk me into believing I was the father of both his fucking kids." Weezy was acting like he had amnesia or some shit, forgetting all the shit that Lena put him through. I was here to remind his weak ass, though.

"You know what? Fuck you, Domino!" He jumped his shrimp cocktail ass up out the chair like he was about to do something. Weezy was the last person on earth that would scare me. He was only five foot eight, and with a wet t-shirt, weighed a buck fifty. That nigga wasn't scaring shit but a squirrel.

"Calm the fuck down, man." I lit a cigar and offered it to him, but he declined it, so I began smoking it. "I'm just saying, you used to wish for days you were out of her house, now you're back? I get that she's sick, but if it was the other way around, would she do that shit for you? You gotta stop giving these hoes the royal treatment. Lena don't deserve shit from you but yo' dick to suck."

He knew I was right. I could tell by the look in his eyes that he knew he'd fucked up by leaving Janay hanging, but that was some shit he'd have to live with. I just wanted him to hear how stupid that shit sounded out loud.

"I know, man. It don't make much sense to you, but it's what I gotta do for right now. This shit ain't forever." Weezy poured some of the liquor in his cup and chugged that shit in one gulp, before continuing. "Oh, and I'll be by to see Baby D soon. I hadn't been able to get up there, given everything going on with Lena, but I've been praying for that nigga. I feel bad 'cuz we had a falling out before it happened, but that's my lil' nigga for life."

"Man, you're the reason he was on that shit. I ain't mad at you for it, 'cuz he's a grown motherfucker, but don't apologize to me for not seeing him. Apologize for getting him addicted to some shit that ain't no good for his ass."

The first thing Davion was gon' do when he got out that fucking coma was go to rehab. I already threw the rest of his stash away, and I didn't give a fuck how he felt about it. The nigga was like a hurricane – always ready to do fucking damage. I needed him to chill, and if this accident didn't calm his ass down, I was gon' be taking matters into my own hands.

"I know, man. It's my fault. But, I wasn't teaching that nigga to be a crackhead. I hope you believe me. He knew about all the shit Lena put me through, and he asked how I dealt with it. He told me he had a lot of stress, and I just showed him what eased my mind. I never thought it would go as far as it did."

My man Weezy was an honest motherfucker, so I nodded my head to show him I believed him. Like I said, the shit wasn't that deep to me, because I had a plan for my brother when he got out the hospital. So, I wasn't tripping.

I dapped Weezy up and enjoyed the rest of my drink. We changed the subject to sports, and by the time we got to the hotel, it was damn near time to open our eyes again to catch the flight home. To my surprise, he didn't even have to use the condoms.

Chapter Nineteen
DAVION "BABY D" BLACK
The next morning...

I could barely open my eyes, because a bright light was beaming down on me. The shit was blinding me. I felt my hands try to move, to block it, but they remained still. I had no idea where I was, or who was here with me. I just knew I was hot and couldn't see. A man with light brown skin took me in his arms and hugged me, and my parents then joined us. My fucking parents?! They left me at the worst possible time, yet here they were...hugging and kissing on me. Just as I opened my mouth to speak to my mom, she closed it and began speaking.

I love you, Baby D. I'm sorry I left you. I didn't want to. But what you're doing down there...it's not acceptable. If I was there, you wouldn't be doing all of this, baby. So don't do it just because I left you. Football isn't everything. Your life is. Your health is. Your family is.

You only have one life, son. You don't want to throw it away. I'll see you again, soon. But let's not make it too soon.

She flew away before I could respond. Where the fuck was she going? Why all them motherfuckers left me at once? I needed another hug. It's been too long since I've had one...

"He's opening his eyes!" I heard someone damn near shout above me. The voice sounded familiar, but I couldn't make out who it belonged to. "Davion? Baby. Can you hear me? It's Camiyah."

Camiyah? I felt a warm hand cover mine, and then a pair of lips on my face. The bright light slowly faded, and I was then able to open my eyes. Slowly, though. That shit was painful.

Turning my head from side to side hurt like a motherfucker. I had to do that shit slowly. Also, I was confused as fuck. I had just been with my parents, and now, I was strapped to a bed. I was in a fucking cold ass hospital room, but that's not where I was supposed to be. Camiyah, my brother Dedrick, and some damn baby were surrounding me. A doctor was smiling at me and talking about me as if I wasn't even in the room.

"Davion may suffer from short term memory loss, because of the accident. He will be paralyzed from the waist down, but there are several things you can do with him to help him regain his memory."

"What? What accident? Paralyzed? No. I'm going to the NFL. What's he talking about, Dedrick? I was just...I was just with mom and dad."

Dedrick shook his head slowly as tears swelled in his eyes.

"I'm sorry, little bro. You must have been dreaming. You were in a car accident over a week ago, and you weren't wearing a seatbelt. Your body was ejected from your car, so you're lucky to be alive. But unfortunately, you won't be able to walk again."

Camiyah kissed my hand. "We're here for you, Davion. Me and your daughter. We'll do all we can to nurse you back to health."

Daughter?

"I don't have any kids, Camiyah. What the fuck? You fucking with me?"

I didn't have time for this bullshit. Didn't they hear me say I was on the football team? I had practice to get to.

Camiyah placed the baby on the bed beside me. "This is Camia, Davion. Camia Diavion Black. Your daughter. You love her very much."

She was cute as hell, I couldn't deny it. "My baby? How old is she?"

"Just three months old."

Three months? Have I been in a coma for three months?

"I don't know what's going on." I was trying to get out of the bed, but my legs weren't working. I couldn't kick them over the bed. I couldn't even feel the motherfuckers. It felt like they were gone. "Am I really paralyzed? What the fuck?" Hot tears streamed down my face as I tried to take all this information in. Why would God give me all this talent just for it to go down the fucking drain? None of this made sense, but I couldn't even move. All I could do was cry.

I couldn't even begin to describe how my body felt. Each time I tried to lift my legs, so I could get out this motherfucking bed, it felt like dead weight. I was numb all over, and I needed an explanation real fucking quick. "Aye you." I looked at the doctor and snapped my fingers. "Tell me what the fuck is going on since you're the one in the white coat. Fuck this bullshit she's on." I wasn't trying to hear nothing Camiyah was saying about no baby; I wanted to know what the fuck was going on with my legs.

The doctor walked over to where I was laying and began speaking. "When you got into the car accident, son, you suffered major blows to the head. A TBI, which is a traumatic brain injury, caused paralysis in your leg muscles, because your brain is no longer communicating with the muscles, telling them to move. Your brain injury is also the reason your short-term memory may be lost for a bit. You'll get that back, eventually."

I shook my head, 'cuz the shit wasn't making sense. One minute, I was perfectly fine, and the next, I wake up in a hospital bed and I can't move my fucking legs.

The doctor nodded his head and continued. "I'm sorry, son – "

"I'm not your fucking son. That much I do remember. My parents are gone man. They just fucking flew away!" I was yelling and crying, which in turn made my head hurt. But, all these fucking emotions would do that to any motherfucker. "You refer to me as Mr. Black, my nigga. You got it?" I always made sure crackers showed me respect. Calling me "boy" and "son"...that shit wasn't gon' fly with me.

His face was pale as fuck, like a vampire, but it turned as red as a bitch's period blood. "I'm sorry, *Mr. Black*. We can get you with a physical therapist, and they may be able to help you regain your strength in your legs, but the chances of you playing football again are...extremely, extremely low."

Without another word, he left the room, and I let out crazy screams and yells. What the fuck was I going to do without football? This shit was like a nightmare that I wanted to wake from, as soon as possible. All my life, I'd been conditioning for the NFL. A professional quarterback was all I wanted to be. I'd been busting my ass on the field and in the locker room since the age of four, and now, at fucking eighteen-years-old, I'm supposed to just give up? Nah, this ain't right. This ain't right at all, and everybody in this motherfucking hospital was gon' feel my rage!

Later that day...

My parents still haven't come back to me, and that shit was pissing me the fuck off. I guess Dedrick was right – I'd been dreaming. That shit felt so real, though. Too real. And my mom's words were stuck in my head. Crazy how she told me football wasn't everything right before I got the worst fucking news ever about my legs. I wanted to fuck the doctor up for what he told me, but in reality, I couldn't bust a grape in a fruit fight right now. Not being able to move my legs was weird as fuck.

Every time one of these dumb ass doctors or nurses came in, I'd asked them if what that white nigga said was true. And all of 'em were pissing me off, because they said yes. All I wanted to do was sleep, because when I was asleep, none of this shit mattered. But when I opened my eyes, I got angry and depressed all over. I wanted to choke the fuck out of someone, but I couldn't get out of bed to do it.

This was one of the rare moments none of the hospital staff was in here checking on me, and I appreciated having them out of my fucking face for the time being. The motherfuckers acted like they couldn't go a second without poking me and asking how I felt. How the fuck am I supposed to feel? How would you feel if someone told you that the one thing you wanted to do with your life, you could never do? How would you feel if you woke up one day and couldn't move the most important muscles in your body? This shit is sick, man.

"You want some water, baby?" Camiyah asked, while laying the baby in bed with me.

I nodded my head and she got up to pour me some water. She even put the straw to my lips, so all I had to do was sip.

"I know you got some devasting news earlier – "

"No shit, Sherlock." I snapped, finishing the water. Shit was beyond devastating. I couldn't even explain the hurt.

"But," she continued. "The good thing is that you'll be

okay. You're not dead, which is great for Camia, because you're such a great father to her."

"I am?"

I guess this was the memory loss shit the doctor spoke about. Most shit, I remembered, but shit like what I was doing before the accident, I didn't. And I damn sure didn't remember being a father. But, Camiyah had shown me pictures and shit of me and Camia, so I guess that shit was true. Maybe that was why in my dream, my mom told me that my family was important. I never wanted kids, but maybe she was telling me to be a good one to my daughter. Damn...she never got to meet her first grandchild. I swear it wasn't supposed to be like this.

Camiyah kissed me on the forehead, interrupting my thoughts, then squeezed my hand. "Yes, baby. You're a wonderful father to Camia, and all I want is for us to continue growing, as a family. Now that you may not play football again, some people might turn their backs on you. But us... we're here forever. We're a family."

I didn't remember agreeing to that shit either. I knew Camiyah was a stripper I'd hit a few times, but having an actual relationship with her did not jog my memory. I guess it was cool, though, 'cuz she was there for a nigga. She hadn't left my side since I got word about my legs today, and I appreciated her for holding me down. I never really cared to have a steady female, because bitches were always disposable, but right now, a nigga needed somebody. I felt like shit, man. I didn't even feel like I had a reason to live. But my mom was right – I needed to do better. My memory was shot according to the doctor, but I do remember leaning on pills, weed, and other drugs to ease my mind about all the bullshit life threw at me. It seemed like my mom wanted me to quit that shit. I probably needed to. It just…it made a nigga feel so good. So relaxed. With all the bullshit I've been going through, without my medicine, as I called it, I wouldn't be able to survive.

Just as that thought crossed my mind, Camia crawled on my chest and laid there. I never thought I could feel this way about a kid, but my heart was pounding fast as hell, and it felt full. Maybe she was my reason to survive? I couldn't tell yet, 'cuz this was still so new to me. I just didn't know what to do with a fucking baby. I was used to being the baby, man. How was I supposed to look after someone else? Times like this, I needed my fucking parents.

She kept lifting her head to look at me, so I did what I thought was right, and kissed her. When I kissed her on the top of her lil' round ass head, the way she giggled and smacked her lil' lips together made me feel good inside. I don't know…it was just a feeling that I couldn't explain.

Chapter Twenty
DOMINO BLACK

That shit that went down at Bailee's shop last week still had me tight as a motherfucker, I just haven't had much time to act on it. The moment she told me it was some old nigga in a Steve Harvey suit I knew who it was, but the paper he'd dropped out of his suitcase when he went running out the door like a lil' bitch confirmed it. His name was in the top left corner, in black, bold letters. James Montclair. That old ass nigga was about to get his shit rocked.

I didn't know what this nigga's deal was with me, but that shit had to be more than him wanting to do business. He was trying too motherfucking hard to get me to sign some papers, so I decided to a do a little research on my own and get the shit popping. People loved to think 'cuz I was in my twenties and a hood nigga that I was dumb. I was far from it. That nigga wanted smoke, so I was bringing the grill.

I still had his number from when he hit me up on Instagram before our initial meeting, so I hit that nigga up and told him I wanted to accept his offer. Of course his pussy ass fell for it, and he was currently pulling up at the abandoned house I sent him the address to. Well, this motherfucker wasn't really abandoned, 'cuz anytime my boys and I needed to do some fucked up shit, we'd use this spot.

"Nice to see you, Domino. I'm glad you finally are ready to accept my offer. Perhaps, we should be meeting at The Black Palace, instead, though, shouldn't we?" His goofy ass was standing at the door cheesing, but that smile faded the minute I put my pistol to his head.

"Nah, motherfucker. I ain't accepting shit. Get your bitch ass in here." I pushed him inside the house, where my niggas were already there, waiting to dispose of his body. I didn't know what the fuck they did with these bodies when I gave 'em to them, nor did I care. I paid them to make sure the murders never linked back to me, and they haven't let me down yet.

"What's going on? Mr. Black, I thought you wanted to – "

"Save it!" I barked and smacked the fuck out of his meaty ass head with the gun. The back of that nigga's head looked like a pack of eight hot dogs. "I know what you're trying to do, and you failed. Motherfucking old ass nigga, built like Spongebob Squarepants with fucking rolls in his neck, trying to play me? You must not know I pack more heat than hell."

After all the research I'd done regarding this nigga, I

finally found out the reason he was after me. My dad owed him some money, and never was able to pay it back. This loan shark motherfucker must've thought that he was gon' get that shit back from me. Oh fucking well.

"Domino, I wasn't – "

Pow!

I was tired of hearing his pussy ass speak. He wasn't about to do shit but lie anyway, and I had better shit to do than listen to him. I fired another shot, just to make sure he was gone. That nigga's brain was splattered everywhere, so I told my niggas to take his body. Before they slid him away, I grabbed his cell phone. Just as I'd thought, he was fucking Tatianna. That bitch was next on my list, and I couldn't promise I was going to take it easy on her plotting, ruthless ass.

One hour later...

I only knew where Tatianna lived, 'cuz she'd always bragged about living in these expensive ass condos, as if anybody gave a fuck where she lived. Her shit wasn't fucking with mine, by a long shot. I could sit five of these condos in the first floor of my crib, and still have room to spare.

It was after hours, so I was able to break into the office downstairs of her building and find which condo was hers. When I got to her condo, I knocked hard on the door.

"Baby! Is it you?"

I didn't say shit. Instead, I knocked hard as fuck, again. I had my thumb covering the peephole, preventing her from seeing who the fuck it was.

"I've missed you so much, ba...Domino! What an...what an interesting surprise." Tatianna opened the door and stretched her arm out, offering me to come in. "You can come on in. Can I offer you a drink, some food...anything?"

When Tatianna said the word 'anything', she ran her fingers across the front of her box, as if to offer me some pussy. From what I remember, that shit looked like an opened can of sardines, so I was offended that she was trying to throw that shit at me. The shit would probably run away if it could.

"I don't want none of your busted down food, drinks, or pussy. What I wanna know is, do you wanna be cremated or buried?"

"What?" She laughed nervously while looking at me like she was confused. "You're so funny, Domino." She licked her crusty lips, trying to be sexy, but that shit was a fail. "You know you came over here because Bailee wasn't doing it for you anymore...I know you want a more experienced woman. You remember the head I gave you in Miami?"

"I remember how whack that shit was. You ain't even made me buss; shit, my hand fucks me better than that." I drew my gun and told her to untie her robe. "And make it quick."

"Is this your idea of foreplay? I can dig it." Tatianna smiled and twirled as she removed her pink silk robe, and the moment she was facing me butt ass naked, I shot her right in the pussy. That ugly shit. Hell, it looked like it would've shot me first, had I not shot it. I hated ugly pussies, man. That shit was in panties or clothing all day, so it had no need to not to look decent when it was time to be fucked.

I called my boys to come handle her, and I left. She wanted to use that tree bark looking ass pussy so much, I'd like to see her try, now. Dead ass bitch.

One week later...

Shit had been going copacetic lately. Davion was out of the hospital, and at my parents' crib where Camiyah was helping to take care of him. He was going to physical therapy, too. Three days a week. Nobody knew if he'd be able to walk again, but that lil' motherfucker was determined, so I didn't say shit to stop him. I was just happy I hadn't seen him do drugs or even pick up a beer since the accident. I didn't even have to send the lil' nigga to rehab; he quit on his own. I knew it was gon' take a lot for his hard-headed ass to learn, but I wasn't expecting his ass to figure it out so soon. I was proud of the nigga.

Bailee was doing the damn thing with her shop, decorating and getting ready for the grand opening; I was proud of my shorty. Bitches rarely ever impressed me, but mine found a way to every single day. I could've had a bitch had did nothing but sit on her ass on all day, ordering bundles and shit, but nah, I had one who wanted to hustle just like me. Shit, the fact that she was carrying my seed made me love her even more. I couldn't believe I was gon' be a father, man. That shit had me hyped as hell. Whether the kid looked like me or Bai, it was gon' be cute as fuck and not one to be fucked with. I wasn't about to raise no motherfucking punk ass kids, so I was gon' teach him or her everything I knew. The same father my dad was to me, was the one I was gon' be to my seed, and I knew Bailee was gon' be one hell of a mom. There wasn't a bitch in the world better than her to carry my child.

Her fine ass was lying in bed beside me, letting me massage her ass, which was getting fatter by the day. Everything about her seemed sexier, now that she was my fiancé and my baby's mama.

"You're so nasty, baby." She giggled, as my finger entered her bootyhole. I told my bitch a while ago that no spot on her was off limits, and I meant that. Everything on Bailee's fucking body was mine, and if she didn't like it, well, she could just go get a new body.

"I'm a nasty ass nigga, but you like it." I pulled her on top of me, wrapping her thick legs across my body. My girl never wore panties anymore, so I had full access to that cookie. Bailee pulled my erect dick out of my basketball shorts and slid it in her pussy. It was amazing how I'd fucked this girl damn near every day, yet her shit was always tight as fuck and dripping wet. Her pussy was made for my meat; I was convinced.

Once she found her rhythm, Bailee rocked her hips in a circular motion, filling that pretty little pussy up with my joint. I bounced her on my dick hard as he dug her nails in my back, screaming my name. She creamed all over my dick, then fell asleep in my arms for the rest of the night.

Chapter Twenty-One
WEEZY
The next morning...

Although Domino reassured me it wasn't my fault, I was still fucked up in the head about Baby D, man. I called Dom this morning and found out he was back home, which was a blessing, but I felt bad for not being there for him during his time of need. And to make matters worse, I had no idea when I'd be able to come around and see him, 'cuz Lena was declining by the day. And the fucked up thing about it was that her attitude was still nasty as fuck toward me. Had me wondering why the fuck I was even here, but I knew she was scared and didn't feel well, so despite my self-esteem dwindling like fuck, I couldn't do shit about it. I didn't even have time to go to see my fucking therapist, 'cuz there was always an appointment Lena had, or somewhere the kids had to go.

Ding! Ding!

That was the bell Lena begged me to get, so I'd know when she needed me. Which was all the goddamn time.

Her breathing was becoming slower, due to the shortness of breath caused by Sarcoidosis, so it took a lot out of her to call my name. Oddly enough, her motherfucking ass wasn't hurting too bad when it came to talking to me like she was crazy, which was exactly what she'd done the moment I entered the room.

"About time you brought your ass in here. I'm dying, Renard. I need water. Fetch it for me."

This bitch was really talking to me like I was a fucking dog, man. And, a motherfucking please would be nice. But I guess that was too much to ask of Lena. She was a real pain in my ass.

I poured her some water from the pitcher I'd left in her room. Truthfully, she could've gotten that shit herself, because I sat it on the dresser. But, like most women would do, she was soaking this shit up.

"You know I have an appointment at noon, right? I know you better be taking me."

I glanced at the clock and it was 11:12 a.m. I haven't even showered yet, and I wanted to take some time and check in with Dom, too. Honestly, I felt bad 'cuz I'd abandoned The Black Palace, and that was wrong as hell, considering he gave me the job as a handout to get myself right.

"Problem?" Lena asked, sipping her water. She then coughed so fucking loud that some white shit came flying out her mouth.

"Man, Lena! Watch where the fuck you hawking your shit!" It landed right on my damn shirt. My good shirt, too. This shit was Gucci.

"Boy!" Lena damn near hopped up out the bed and jacked me up by the collar. For a bitch that was terminally ill, she wasn't acting like she was sick. "Don't you ever talk to me like that again, you limp dick motherfucker! I'll hawk my spit in your mouth if I feel like it!"

I fell back as she let me go, and then she did just as she promised and hawked spit at my mouth. "Now get ready, Weezy. I have a fucking appointment, and if I'm late, I swear you'll die before me."

With tears in my eyes, I left the room, slamming the door behind me. I needed my therapist. I needed something to smoke. And most of all, I needed Janay.

One hour later...

"Your disease is worsening, Lena. I hate to tell you, but with your vision getting blurrier, I believe the sarcoidosis is causing a case of glaucoma. On top of that, your cough...your lungs are weakening. Are you still smoking?"

"No." Lena lied, looking the doctor right in his eyes. "Fix this shit, doctor. I can't leave *him* to raise my kids. He can't even get me to these appointments on time."

We were only eight minutes late, and it was because she wanted to stop at the gas station for a pack of cigarettes.

The doctor looked at both of us and shook his head. You

could tell his ass was uncomfortable and ready to get us the fuck out of his office. "I wish I had better news, Lena. We've been dealing with this for almost five years now, and usually while sarcoidosis has the potential to get better...I'll be honest. In African-Americans, the mortality rate is higher. And given all the other outside factors, like stress, diet, lack of exercise, and tobacco use, we didn't fight it as much as we could."

It was still crazy to me that she knew she had this since 2013. Maybe had she told me back then, we could've changed things and saved her life. Now, I didn't give a fuck. Lena was getting meaner by the minute, and I knew it was because she taking her fear out on me, but after today, that would no longer be an option.

As soon as the doctor left, I rolled Lena out to the car, and she showed her first sign of emotion since the night she told me. She broke down crying in the car.

"I'm so happy you're here with me, Weezy. I'm glad it was you at that appointment instead of the kids. They didn't need to hear that."

Speaking of the kids, we needed to talk. "Lena, I got some shit to ask you, alright?" I handed her a tissue from the glove compartment before driving off. "So, you know I had a DNA test taken for the kids, right?" She nodded her head slowly. "Well, guess what the fuck I found out?" I didn't give her a chance to speak before I dived in again. I was getting heated just thinking about that trifling ass information. "Jay is mine, but Kay isn't. Which means you were fucking around within the same few days as you were fucking me. Can you explain that to me, Lena?"

"I ain't explaining shit." She snapped, drying her eyes. "You did what you did, and so did I. Guess who signed her birth certificate, bitch? You!" She knocked me upside the head while I drove, which caused me to speed the fuck up.

I didn't even respond to her. I drove her the fuck home, put her sick ass back in the bed, and did something I should've done a long fucking time ago – left! Fuck her illness, man!

When I got back in the car, I called Janay nonstop 'til she finally answered.

"What, Weezy? I'm busy. I'm working."

"Where? Kroger?" I was hoping she wasn't dancing for anybody, because today would be the day I'd go to jail for murder. I was determined to get my girl back.

Instead of answering, she asked, "Why?"

That told me all I needed to know. "I'm on my way."

I got to her store within the next fifteen minutes, and the second I laid my eyes on her, I felt stupid as fuck for leaving her to go back to Lena. Maybe it was because I hadn't seen her in a while, but she looked more beautiful than I remembered her before, even though she was wearing a scowl on her face.

After she checked out the customer in her line, I put up the 'closed' sign just as the next family walked up. "She'll be back. Go to the next cashier, y'all." I grabbed her hand and led her outside.

"Weezy, are you trying to get me fired? Why are you here? I thought you were fucking with Le-".

I shut her up with a kiss, wrapping my arms around her back and caressing her slim waist and fat ass. Damn, I missed these lips. My manhood throbbed uncontrollably as I pressed myself against her. "Come with me, baby. Please."

"No, Renard. You left me for your wife. How do I know that won't happen again?"

Just as she said that, my phone rang, and Lena's name flashed across the screen. Before Janay could say shit about it, I ignored the call. Lena called two more times, and I ignored the other calls, too.

"See? That's how you know, baby. I'm all yours. Fuck her. I wanna be with you, Janay."

"If you wanna be with me, Weezy...that means being with me. Not just when it's convenient for you. And it also means accepting me. I appreciate those clothes you got me, but realize I don't have the money to keep myself up like that."

"But I do." I removed her Kroger apron from around her waist. "Let me take care of you, Janay. All your life, you've been taking care of people. Helping your mom with her bills, paying for shit for your siblings...let me help you. Quit this job, baby. And the other one. I got you."

"I can't put my trust in a man, Renard."

"You damn right you can't. But in *your* man, you can."

That got a smile out of her. I told her to go in and tell her manager she quit, then to come back to my car. While I waited for her, Lena's number flashed across my screen again.

This time I answered, but I was gon' set shit straight with her ass, so she'd know I wasn't her lil' bitch boy anymore.

"What, Lena? What the fuck do you want? I don't know why you're calling me, 'cuz I should've been through with your ass the moment I found out Kayden ain't mine!"

"What?"

That wasn't Lena's voice.

"Who's this?" I asked, as my heart raced.

I heard nothing was screams and sobs from the other end. "Daddy, it's me...Kayden....mommy's dead. Are you not my daddy? What? I hate you! I just want my mom!"

Click.

I couldn't believe this shit, man. In one second, my kids had lost their fucking mother...but I'd also lost my fucking kid.

Chapter Twenty-Two
BAILEE RODGERS
That same day...

I was a nervous fucking wreck. Today was my state board test to become a licensed cosmetologist, and although I knew that I knew my shit, I was antsy.

"Come here, baby. You look nervous. You know you gon' pass that fucking test, and if you don't, I'ma change all the fucking right answers to the shit you put down, so it looks like you passed." Dom sat a plate of breakfast he'd cooked in front of me, and began feeding me the eggs first, since he knew they were my favorite. He'd been doing that a lot lately, since I learned of my pregnancy. Feeding me, catering to me...doing everything he could to make sure I was comfortable, and I loved him for that. But today, I didn't think Jesus himself could calm my nerves.

"Thank you, baby. I hope so. These eggs are the fucking

bomb, by the way." I ate more off the fork. "The baby must really like them."

"My son don't like no nasty ass eggs. Real niggas eat meat, not that fucking bird food." He rubbed my belly, which was no longer completely flat; I wasn't big, either. It just looked like I'd eaten a heavy lunch.

"What makes you think it's a boy, Domino? This very well might be little Brielle in here."

"Nah, I remember the night I got you pregnant. I laid it the fuck down. I made a man that night, who gon' do the same shit to his bitch one day."

I rolled my eyes and laughed. We were far away from finding out the sex of the baby, but after my state board exam, we did have our first doctor's appointment. Hopefully we'd get to have an ultrasound done, because I was ready to see my little peanut on the screen.

Dom's phone rang, and when he answered it, all he did was laugh. That shit had me curious, so of course I asked him who it was.

"It was Weezy. That fat bitch Lena, she finally died."

My heart sank. I wasn't a fan of hers at all, because she was a terrible person toward Weezy. But, I was at least hoping she'd beat her illness, for her children's sake.

"But, didn't you laugh?" I asked, finishing my breakfast.

"Yep. Shit, it was about fucking time. Nobody wanted that bitch alive, anyway. Maybe now Weezy can be a fucking man."

He could be so harsh, but for some reason, I couldn't get enough of his brashness. That's why so many people were skeptical of our relationship, because it was a known fact that the nigga was mean as hell. The only person he treated with respect was me.

After eating, Domino wished me luck for the test in the form of giving me some amazing oral sex, and then I made my way to the testing center. The caterpillars in my stomach turned into full-fledged butterflies as I walked through the door. I said a silent prayer to the Man Upstairs, because this was the last piece in the puzzle to making my dreams come true.

Later that day...

I passed! I knew I would, but I guess I didn't want to be overconfident and end up under delivering. But, I didn't. I did it! Next up was graduation, which was next week, and then to plan the grand opening of my salon. Life was good!

Now that I had that taken care of, I was heading to the doctor's office for my very first pregnancy appointment. Domino was going to meet me there, but he'd texted me to let me know he'd be late due to having to handle something via phone with Jerrod about the Miami location.

Walking in the doctor's office, the first person I spotted was that bitch, Tierra. I knew she'd been posting shit about being pregnant by Domino, but he showed me the ultrasound she sent him, showing another girl's name, so hopefully she was just here for a check-up.

As soon as I sat my ass down in the seat to complete my paperwork, Tierra came to sit beside me.

"Why are you sitting over here? That seat is for Domino, and you know he'll throw you out the window, next, if he catches you in my presence." Dom told me he threw her puppy out the window, which was crazy as hell. That man had no chill.

Running her fingers through the little bit of hair she had, Tierra laughed. "I'm not here checking for you, if that's what you're thinking." She crossed her legs, kicking her blue knock-off Manolo boots in the air. "I do go to the doctor, just like any other woman. Why are you here? Are you pregnant?"

"Yep." I continued filling out my paperwork.

"He's gonna do the same thing to you that he did to me. Just warning you. And did you know he killed my dog?"

I laughed, because Domino did, in fact, tell me he threw her puppy out the window. That was her fault, because she was trying to fake a pregnancy with the wrong nigga. She knew just as well as I did that Domino was off his rocker.

"Like I said, he's gonna do you the same way." Tierra cocked her head and smirked, trying to get a reaction out of me.

"That's where you're wrong, bitch." I got loud on her ass; obviously she wanted a show, so the bitch was gon' get one today. "You were just a fuck to Domino. That's why he had no problem taking you to the mental hospital, or breaking your foot with his Timberland, or throwing your ugly ass dog out the window. You know what he does for me? That man runs me baths, cooks for me, makes sure I never touch a gas pump, and fucks me 'til I'm speaking in tongues. Every night. And a bitch like you couldn't take him off my hands if I paid you." I stood over her, looking her right in the fucking eyes. "If you ever disrespect me again, the moment I drop this baby, I'm dropping you on your ass, alright? Don't fuck with me, Tierra. Me and you...we're in two separate leagues. Stay in your lane, bitch." I held up my left hand. "You and I both know Domino Black wouldn't give this to a bitch he planned on leaving, so you and all his other groupies can kiss my ass. I'm sorry but this isn't Burger King – you won't be having Domino your way."

Her face was stuck on stupid, and I dared her to say another word.

"Bailee Rodgers?" The nurse called my name just as I finished reading Tierra's ass.

"Me." I raised my hand and walked in her direction. "Perfect timing." The only thing missing was Domino, but he'd be here soon enough.

Twenty minutes later...

"I'm the fucking father, man. Y'all ugly motherfuckers gon' let me through! My dick made that baby she's about to look at on the screen. That's my cum all in my bitch's pussy, and if y'all don't let me through, I'ma own this motherfucker by tomorrow."

I chuckled to myself, hearing all the commotion Domino

was making outside the door. He was so embarrassing, but he definitely had a way of getting what he asked for. Within seconds, the doctor came in with him right behind her.

"I was told this is the baby's father? I assume it's okay for him to be back here?" She asked, staring at both Domino and me.

"Okay for me to be back here? Bitch, I be all up in her pussy every single night; you ain't about to see nothing on her body I hadn't fucked. Let me the fuck in."

I shot him a look that said, 'relax', but there was no use. He sat his ass down right in the doctor's seat, leaving her standing.

She left the room while I undressed, and Domino instantly started playing with my pussy the moment my leggings were off. "Stop, baby. We're at the doctor's office." I giggled and moaned, loving the way his fingers felt inside of me. I couldn't deny it – the man had the ability to make me cum just by fingering me for a few seconds. Hell, who was I kidding? He made my panties drenched just by looking at me.

Dipping in and out of my opening, he then removed his fingers and slid in his tongue.

"Ooohhh," I groaned, as he folded his tongue and flicked it across my bud. Eating me as if I was The Last Supper, he kissed my lower lips repeatedly while swiping his tongue over my clit. I felt myself nearing my peak just as the door flew open.

"Give us five more minutes. She's about to cum." Dom pushed the doctor back out the door. He immediately went back to work, thrashing my insides with every flick of his tongue. I shivered as he left no area of my pussy unscathed. I moaned each time he dipped his tongue in and out of my hole. As he sucked on my g-spot, I rode his face in a fast motion, feeling the orgasm build up.

Once my juices rained on his tongue, he brought the doctor back in. I couldn't believe her ass was actually waiting outside the door, but I guess she knew better than to play with my crazy ass fiancé.

She inserted the cold instrument into my vagina, and Dom and I stared at the screen, wondering which spot our baby was.

"Oh yeah, it's a boy. That's his dick right there. He got a big one like me." Dom laughed, pointing at a spot on the screen.

"That's actually your baby's limb." The doctor chuckled. "He or she is still too small for us to know the sex, yet. But, I can tell you, there's a very strong heartbeat and you look really good. Your due date is estimated to be July 31, 2019."

"Oh hell no!" I shouted, while Dom laughed. "That's his birthday! You mean I'm having a Leo that could possibly have the same birthday as their daddy?"

"You'll have to deal with two of me, baby. Forever. Don't worry, the next time I fill your eggs, we might create a girl. But she ain't gon' be no punk bitch. So you'll really be dealing with three Dominos."

Lord help me.

Chapter Twenty-Three
DAVION "BABY D" BLACK

My life had become one boring motherfucker, man. All I did everyday was watch ESPN and hear what they had to say about me. Then, I'd cry. And I wasn't even the emotional type. But everything that had happened within the past few weeks had made me this way. I couldn't control the shit. One minute I was pissed the fuck off, and the next I was back to normal. Whatever the fuck my 'normal' was.

I did take Camiyah's advice and start seeing a therapist. That shit wasn't helping a lot, but it was cool to have someone besides Camiyah to talk to. I mean, I had my brothers, but they didn't understand a nigga. And all my old teammates and shit, they were doing their own things. Nobody took the time to check on me, and that was fucked up. But according to my therapist, I shouldn't expect anybody to. That shit was ludicrous though, because what the fuck was the point in having family and friends if the motherfuckers didn't understand you, fuck with you, or give a fuck about your well-being? On my life, I won't be that type of dad to Camia. Or that type of boyfriend to Camiyah. They were all I had at this point, and I promised myself I'd take care of them. I got their backs.

Looking down at my legs, I began to cry. Not being able to get up and walk where I wanted to was so hard for me. The only bright side to this shit was that my dick wasn't affected and I could still fuck. I just hoped Camiyah's pussy didn't get boring to me, 'cuz who the fuck I'ma bag in a wheelchair?

Physical therapy was helping me learn how to maneuver around a little bit, but I was starting to accept the fact that I'd probably never be on that field again as a player, even if I did regain feeling in my legs and learn how to walk. Before this lil' incident, I took shit like walking and driving for granted – never thought it could be taken away from me. Crazy how shit could change your life within a matter of seconds. All over some stupid shit, too. Apparently, I'd been arguing with Dom and when I got in the car, was too busy trying to roll a blunt that I didn't notice a big ass truck was coming.

It was so hard to accept that I'd fucked my life up, but one thing that helped me cope was little Camia. Whenever I had the urge to get back on the field, or whenever I got down about the situation, Camia's lil' cute ass would come crawling to me, smiling, and those feelings would go away.

Right now, she was lying on my chest sleeping as I flipped

through the channels. I almost threw the remote at the fucking TV when I got to the ESPN channel. They were talking about a nigga, bad. Stephen A. Smith was talking hard cash shit, saying how my supposedly bad attitude would've been my downfall had the accident not happened.

"Man, fuck you! Pussy ass bitch! I hope your mom gets raped with an AIDS dick!" I threw the remote at the TV, cracking the screen. That nigga had me fucked up, man! Most of my memory was back, and yeah, I know not a lot of people didn't fuck with me, but I can't seem to find a fuck to give. Swear to God, if my legs moved, I'd be fucking disrespectful niggas like him up on sight!

"What's wrong, baby?" Camiyah came into the den, carrying a plate full of steak, loaded mashed potatoes, and green beans. She looked at the TV and her mouth fell open. "Davion! You cracked the TV!"

"I know. And that Stephen A. Smith motherfucker better be glad it wasn't his face." I accepted the plate from her as she took Camia off my chest.

"You can't worry about what people say about you, Davion. You can't control their opinions. The only things that you should be worried about are – "

Ding!

Her sentence was interrupted by the doorbell. She placed Camia back on my chest and went to get the door, and all I heard was bickering.

"Who the fuck is that?" I called out, just as Camiyah walked in, with someone trailing behind her. It was Shanay. I didn't know which I was surprised to see more – her or that big ass belly. Swear I needed my feet to work, so I could kick that bitch down a flight of stairs. "Fuck is you doing here, bitch?"

"My parents were trying to make me have an abortion, but I refused. So, I left California." She said that shit like I was supposed to care.

"Fuck that got to do with me?" I wanted to slap that bitch so hard she landed right back in California, but she'd have to bend down so I could, since I wasn't in my wheelchair. Being paralyzed was a motherfucker!

Camiyah grabbed Camia and gave me a passionate kiss on the lips before leaving the room. She probably did that shit to show Shanay that I was hers, but there was no need for all that. Nobody wanted this little ass kid. I was surprised she was old enough to have a fucking period already. Damn man, how the fuck did I let this giant toddler fool me?

Rolling her eyes at Camiyah, Shanay sat down on the couch beside me, but I pinched her ass cheek hard as hell, making her jump back up. "Don't sit your ugly ass on my couch."

"I'm ugly now? I wasn't ugly when you were moaning my name." She threw her head back and laughed, so I yanked that fucking ponytail made out of horse hair from out of her head. Shit looked like a goddamn raccoon. "Davion! Why would you do that?"

"Why the fuck you here, yo? I got my own shit I'm dealing with, and it don't include you!" I pointed to my wheelchair, which was right beside the couch. "Keep fucking playing with me, and I won't be the only one who needs that motherfucker!"

"Davion, can you just hear me out?"

"Ain't shit you can say to me, Shanay. What you should've said was that you were fuckin' fourteen years old, but since you couldn't say that much, don't say shit to me. Get your ass out." I threw her ponytail at her.

Tears filled her eyes. "Davion. I told my parents I love you. We love each other. I want to have this baby, and I want us to be a family. Can I stay here? I have nowhere to go."

"Bitch, are you blind or mentally retarded? Did my bitch not just answer the fucking door for you? I wouldn't let you stay in my garbage can, let alone my house."

Rubbing her belly, she tried to sit down for a second time, but I pinched her again.

"Davion! I'm your baby's mother. How could you treat your child like this?"

"Fuck you and that baby. The only child I have is Camia." I wasn't claiming no baby by an underage bitch. I wasn't no fucking cradle robber, man. Who the fuck she thought I was? Michael Jackson?

"You're making a mistake, Davion." She stood up and headed for the door just as Camiyah and Camia came back in the den.

Grabbing Camia from her mom, I laughed and said, "The only mistake I made was not checking behind your ears for your mama's spoiled titty milk, bitch. Baby, let her out."

Camiyah walked her to the door while I held my *real* child in my arms. I kissed her plump lil' cheeks and blew on her stomach, 'cuz that shit always made her cute ass laugh. Camia was cute as fuck, man.

Camiyah joined us on the couch, once Shanay was gone. As I played with my kid, she rubbed my back and fed me the rest of my dinner. This was how a man was supposed to be treated...

The next day...

While Camiyah was at work, I spent my days with Camia, and I loved every bit of it, man. She was growing so much, and I didn't want to miss a minute of being with her. I actually hated times like this, when she was napping.

But, her naptime did give me time to myself, which I needed like fuck, since the news outlets treated my name like a dick – it was always in their mouths. It seemed like everybody was praying on my downfall. I was gon' show them motherfuckers, though.

Since I had an ass of free time now, I'd been doing research to see how I could still do sports related shit. I found out that Nike was actually running a campaign about people with disabilities still able to play sports, and since I was now in a wheelchair, I wanted to take a shot at it. I mean, all I damn near wore was Nike, and I was the top recruit in the country when I was in high school, so who would be better for the job? There was nobody who should be the face of Nike except me.

I just had to convince these crackers of that. And that's who I was on the line with, now. Well, on hold.

Ding!

I didn't want to answer the doorbell, because the last visitor I got was that high school bitch. If it was her again, I was liable to choke the fuck out of her with that raccoon she used for a ponytail.

Whoever the fuck it was rang the bell again, and since I didn't want them to wake up lil' mama just yet, I wheeled to the front door and answered it.

"Who the fuck is you, bruh?"

It was a tall, lanky, white motherfucker at my door, holding a manilla envelope. "I'm here to deliver a package to Mr. Davion Black."

I grabbed the envelope out of his hand slammed the door in his face. I knew that when motherfuckers arrived at your door with an envelope, it was usually a bullshit ass reason to appear in court. I could only imagine what the fuck this shit was. It seemed like everybody was out to get a nigga.

I started reading the shit and instantly got pissed the fuck off. It said that Celine had issued a restraining order against me, and that if I came within 300 feet of the bitch, I was going to jail. This didn't even seem like some shit she would do, though. This had her pussy ass boyfriend written all over it. I guess they were trying to retaliate for what I did to her car, but fuck her whip, man! She let her nigga lay his hands on me, so I had to teach her a lesson!

I ripped the fucking paper up and wheeled over to the counter in the kitchen where I kept my car keys. It then dawned on me that I couldn't fucking drive. Fuck! That lil' Mexican wet back bitch better be glad my legs are fucking paralyzed, 'cuz otherwise, she would've gotten all the enchiladas knocked out of her. I was pissed! The only thing I could do to ease my mind was stroke Camia's back while she slept, 'cuz I had no drugs or pills, nor was I able to go beat that bitch's ass. Damn.

Chapter Twenty-Four
CELINE GOMEZ
A few days later...

It's been a few days since I had the papers served to Davion, and I was proud to say, it's been quiet. I haven't heard nada from him, and for him, and that showed so much maturity that I was actually proud of him. The only reason I'd done it was because I wanted to prove to Eric I had no ties to him. Now that he believed me, our relationship was back to normal, and I couldn't be happier.

I was currently at home, fixing Eric and myself a nice dinner consisting of paella and chorizo. He loved the Spanish rice dish and spicy sausage the last time I cooked it, so I wanted to surprise him with it tonight. Just a way to thank him for all his kindness and patience.

Just as I was removing the pan of paella from the oven, the doorbell rang. I looked at the clock, and as expected, Eric was right on time. "Coming, papi!" I shouted, as I removed my apron and reapplied my lipstick. When I opened the front door, I was highly disappointed. It was some random kid – probably one from the neighborhood, trying to sell something.

"I'm not interested." I attempted to close the door, but he pushed it open.

"You don't even know what I'm giving out, ma. And you're closing the door on a nigga." He laughed, but it sounded like pure evil rolling off his lips. El diablo.

He was standing there, not holding a damn thing, but steadily trying to get in my house. My first instinct told me he was trying to rob me in broad daylight, and I wished Eric would hurry up and get here.

"I said I don't care! Go away!" I pushed him once more.

"My homeboy said to give you this."

Wham!

He punched me in the face and ran away. I had no doubt that my eye was swollen, because he'd socked me pretty hard. Slamming the door behind me and locking it, I dashed to the kitchen to call Eric and tell him what happened. Then, I was going to call the police. He said his homeboy sent him to do that to me, and if that were the truth, I had a gut feeling it was Davion. He just wouldn't leave me alone.

Eric was heated when I called him, and he promised he was on the way. Before I got to dial 9-1-1, the doorbell rang again. I grabbed a frying pan and walked to the door, because if it was him or anyone else trying to give me another hit, I wanted to be prepared. I needed a fucking gun.

I opened the door again, and immediately started beating the guy with the frying pan. "Leave...me...alone! Don't.... come...here...again!"

"It's me, bebita! Stop!"

Bebita? The only person who called me bebita was...

"Arturo?" I lifted the visitor's head and sure enough, it was my brother, Arturo, whom I haven't seen in years. I was ordered by my parents to live my life as if Arturo was dead, since he'd disappointed the family. I loved my brother mucho, but he was on serious drugs and he did crazy things, like steal, just to have the money for them. The drugs he did were worse than the ones Davion did, which is why I was so compelled to help him.

"Arturo, what are you doing here? How did you know where I lived?" I let him in and offered him an ice pack to nurse the bruises I'd put on him with the frying pan.

"You need that ice yourself, bebita. What's wrong with your eye?"

I'd forgotten that I had a black eye. "It's nada. Not as important as you. What's going on?"

We sat on the couch and although I tried to refrain, I reached over and hugged him. I hadn't done this since I was maybe seventeen years old. The past few years had been so hard on me, because I needed my brother. And I was sure he needed me.

"I'm alive. Surprisingly." He laughed, but that wasn't funny. It really was by the grace of God that he was alive, because I've seen drugs take so many people out in less time. Arturo had been on heroine, opiods, cocaine, and ecstasy pills for years. And, he drank like a fish.

"Are you hungry? I made paella and – "

"Where is the motherfucker who hit you, baby?" Eric kicked down the door and came into the den with his gun drawn. Before I could answer, he fired a shot at Arturo, hitting him in the arm.

"No! That's not him! That's my brother!" I ran to his side and held him in my arms as his body spasmed. "Call 9-1-1!"

The next day...
Arturo was going to be okay, thank God. Eric said he didn't have the intent of killing the person who'd hit me; he just wanted to scare them. That's why he was aiming for the arm. Arturo promised not to file any charges, since it was an accident, so Eric was taking care of his medical bills.

Eric had just left the hospital to go to work, leaving me and Arturo there to catch up on old times, since we never really got to. Having time alone with my brother was really nice. We laughed, we cried, and he explained to me the reason he'd shown up out of the blue. Arturo had gotten into some shit with his dealer, and owed him some money. He was wanting to see if I had anything he could borrow, which was why he'd randomly shown up.

"How much do you need, Arturo? Cuanto cuesta?"

"Fifteen hundred, por favor. If I don't give it to him in a week, I'm dead."

That was a lot of money. Way more than I'd anticipated him saying, but since he was mi hermano and I wanted to save his life, I told him I'd do it. Giving him a kiss on the forehead, I told him I'd go to the ATM to get the cash while he rested. I planned to get the guy's address and take it over there for him, because I didn't want Arturo having anymore dealings with him.

I felt a presence behind me, as I stood at the hospital's ATM, and when I turned around, I realized who it was.

"Are you stalking me?" I asked Davion.

"Nope, but I see you got my lil' message today." Davion pointed to my eye, which was no longer black, but obviously swollen.

So the guy who hit me...he really *was* sent by him. Wow.

"I did, and I don't fucking appreciate it." I pushed him, and since he was in a wheelchair, he couldn't do shit. "I want you to leave me alone, Davion. Seriously. I'm not interested in you. Te odio."

He laughed like I was telling a joke, and rolled closer to me. "I don't want your ass, honestly. I'm here for physical therapy, not to get you back. I don't even want your ass back, you Taco Bell eating bitch. You were a piece of pussy, and that shit wasn't even hitting on much. I've had better. Your shit was musty like a dirty Mexican restaurant."

His insults were muy divertido. That's how I knew I was over him, because I wasn't bothered by his words anymore.

"Then why the fuck won't you leave me alone?"

If my pussy wasn't so good, he had no reason to be worried about me, right?

"I just wanted to get your stupid ass back for that restraining order. Let me tell you something, J. Ho. You ain't shit to me. You ain't shit to nobody. And that whack ass nigga you fucking…he ain't shit neither. And you can tell him part two is coming real soon; just wait 'til I get out this chair."

"I'd like to see you try." I chuckled because it was quite obvious he was jealous over what I had with Eric. I guess he felt threatened, but that's because Eric was a real man, and Davion could sense that.

When he realized he wasn't getting a rise out of me, Baby D turned around in his chair and wheeled off. I saw the chick Camiyah, and his baby, waiting for him on the other end of the lobby. Although most people might've felt some type of way about his words, I didn't. I felt relieved. He claimed he didn't want me, so I was going to believe that. I was tired of Davion and his games, and I was so ready for him to be over me. I sent a quick prayer up to God and los angeles, asking them to please let it be true that he was over me. That would be the greatest gift anyone could give me.

A few days later…
Now that Arturo was out of the hospital, I really wanted him to stay with me. It wasn't just his road to recovery that I was worried about, but it was his safety. He looked

awful; the drugs had definitely done a number on him. Muy triste.

"Why won't you stay here with me, Arturo? You just got out of el hospital and now you're going back to the same life that put you in there! Estupido!"

"It wasn't the drugs that put me in the hospital." He laughed and shook his head, pointing at Eric. "It was your little novio. There's nothing wrong with a little heroin every now and then, chica. Nada."

I wanted to smack him upside the head and tell him how ignorant he sounded, but it would do no good. El es tonto. And not only is he dumb, he's hard-headed and believes that just because he's thirty, he knows more than I do. He seems to forget that I'm the more successful sibling. At age thirty, Arturo doesn't even have a casa to call his own. He stays on the street, in and out of different girls' homes, and in shelters.

Eric grabbed my arm and pushed me behind him. "It's okay, baby. You can't save everyone. That's what you have to realize."

"That's my brother, papi! Mi hermano! It's my job to --"

"If you wanna help me, give me about five hundred dollars, sis. Then I'll be out of your hair. Lo prometo."

Arturo promising to be out of my hair wasn't doing anything for me. I wanted him here. After four years of not seeing or hearing from him, it felt good to have him around. But, Eric was right. I was always trying to save someone. That's exactly how I got wrapped up in Davion. Trying to save him from himself, but I should've been trying to save myself from him.

"Fine, Arturo." I reached in my Michael Kors bag to hand him another wad of cash. It wasn't the five hundred he asked for, but it was a little over three hundred dollars. He'd have to make due.

"Gracias, hermana!" Arturo kissed me on the cheek and ran out the door as quickly as he'd run in the other day. The moment he left, my tears began to fall; I had a strong feeling that I'd never get to see my brother again. Luckily, I had Eric there to console me. He laid my head on his strong chest and stroked my hair as I cried. I cried for Arturo. I cried for Davion. I cried for all those with adicciones a las drogas.

"You can't change who your brother is, Celine. He's a grown man. The only person you can save is yourself." Eric kissed the top of my head and rubbed my cheek. His words were meant to be comforting, but they weren't. Those who'd never seen addiction up close had no idea how hard it was to just let their loved one hang themselves, so I didn't expect him to understand. The best thing he could do for me was hold me close while I prayed that mi hermano would come to his senses and stop throwing his life away, but I wasn't confident that it would happen.

Chapter Twenty-Five
BAILEE RODGERS
One week later...

Today was so important to me, but clearly, my baby didn't give a damn since this morning sickness was currently kicking my ass. Whoever said pregnancy was a beautiful thing lied. My graduation from Kenneth Shuler School of Cosmetology was today, and then tonight was the grand opening of my salon. It was at the grand opening that I was planning to announce my pregnancy. So, I had a full day ahead, and the only way I could see myself surviving was if Domino's seed eased up on me, just for a few hours.

The second I got out of bed, I had to run to the toilet. Dom was in the bathroom brushing his teeth, so he held my hair while I puked.

"You owe me double head for this. Shit, I want you to suck my dick from the back." Dom laughed, as he cleaned up my mess. I'd aimed straight for the toilet, but had gotten a good bit of vomit on the toilet seat and floor, as well.

"Nigga, you're the reason I'm in this predicament." I rolled my eyes and rinsed my mouth with Listerine. The moment the words left my lips, I instantly regretted them. "I'm sorry, baby. I didn't mean it like that." I walked over to kiss him, but he moved back.

"Do not kiss me 'til all that shit is out your mouth, Bailee. You know I don't give a fuck about none of that shit you talk. I'm used to it by now. I just ignore your goofy ass."

I sucked my teeth and laughed. He was right. Lately, I'd been super emotional and just snapping at him for no reason. I guess it was a mixture of the pregnancy hormones, and nervousness about graduation and my grand opening. I wanted everything to go perfectly, but for some reason, I had a feeling there would be drama.

"You didn't invite Davion to the grand opening, did you?" I asked Dom, stripping my clothes for the shower.

"Yeah. Why?" He laughed just as I reached out my hand to hit him. "I'm fucking with you, baby. I know he can't be in the room with that Spanish broad."

"At all." I was serious. Both of them were like firecrackers, and pregnant or not, I would kick both their asses if anything popped off tonight. So, to keep the peace, Davion, Camiyah, and Camia were coming to my graduation, while Celine and Eric were coming to the grand opening, if they could make it. She hadn't confirmed with me yet. "I don't wanna have to fuck them up for ruining my day, Domino. Especially your brother."

"Fuck all of em. Give me some pussy. You've been depriving a nigga. If I ain't love yo' ass, I would've been cheated."

I glanced at the clock, and unless this was a quickie, I was going to be late to graduation. "Dom, can we do it lat – "

"Fuck that." He kissed me, palming my ass like a basketball. "You gon' get this dick now, and you gon' get this dick later. This pussy is mine, ain't it? Let me know if it's not."

"It is," I moaned, as he massaged my breasts.

I then felt his hand spread my legs apart, and by the time he entered himself inside of me, I felt like I was already about to cum. He was right – it had been a few days since the last time we pleasured one another, so my pussy was drenched and tight. I didn't realize how much I'd missed daddy inside of me.

"You...so...fucking...fine," Dom whispered, as his tongue dipped in and out of my mouth while he stroked me slowly.

I closed my eyes to stop the tears from flowing, because it felt *that* damn good. His lips moved from mine down to my neck, which he knew was my spot. He pushed his entire dick in my whole, and since he was working with a rather large package, I quivered as I adjusted to his girth. Lifting me up, he began bouncing me on his dick, and the feeling of his ten-inch pole going in and out of me slowly and steadily made my juices rain on him almost instantly.

"Fuck, Bai. Your shit super wet." He panted, speeding up his pace.

"This is your pussy, baby. I love...I love you so much."

Domino pulled out slowly, then pummeled himself into me. His dick was so big, I could feel it in my stomach.

"I'ma make yo' sexy ass cum again, Bai. I love it when you cum hard on my dick."

Feeling my body convulse, I knew he was right. Another explosion was underway. He repeated his motion, sliding into me slowly but deeply, and we came simultaneously before getting in the shower together.

When I stood in the shower, Domino washed me, then bent down to serve me with some phenomenal head. After sucking another orgasm out of my body, Domino carried me out the shower, dried my body off, and got me dressed for graduation. I checked the time and as predicted, I was late, but I'd rather be late than horny any day.

Later that night...

Graduation was perfect, and now, I was enjoying what was literally the biggest moment of my life. Bailee's House of Beauty was officially open for business, and I had no one to thank but my awesome fiancé for that. Since the baby had been kicking my ass, Dom handled everything for the grand opening – the decorations, the invites, and making sure all my supplies had been ordered.

I haven't had time to interview stylists to work here either, so I had invited all the girls who'd hit me up on Instagram with interest, and told them to drop their portfolios off to me tonight. I'd start conducting interviews tomorrow, and hopefully by Tuesday, we'd be up and running. Given that today was Friday, it didn't leave me much time, so hopefully the baby wouldn't slow me down over the next few days.

I walked around the room, greeting my guests, while Domino and Kris controlled the crowd. This event was not open to the public, so I wanted to make sure nobody wandered in here. So far, so good.

My parents hadn't arrived yet, but I spotted Tasmine and Landon by the table that was set up as a bar.

"You look beautiful sis," Tas complimented me as I hugged her. "That color. It looks amazing on you."

I was wearing a yellow, off-the-shoulder, long sleeved dress that stopped just above my knees, with a pair of nude Giuseppe heels. My hair was parted down the middle, bone straight, so it stopped in the middle of my back.

"Thanks, Tas. You look good, too."

I hugged Landon, but didn't say much to him. Since the night Dom killed Tyler, I haven't been able to stand being in the same room as him. I guess it was the guilt because while the cops still hadn't solved the mystery surrounding his brother's death, I not only knew, but had played a role in it. However, it was because of what Tyler did to me, so I didn't feel awful about it. Anyway, I'd only invited Landon because of my sister, so I didn't spend much time with them.

I excused myself when I saw my parents walk in. I grabbed Domino and he signaled the deejay to turn the music down. Once we had everyone's attention, we asked the waiters to pass around glasses of champagne to everyone.

"I just want to say, thank you for being here." I yelled loudly. The crowd was excited, which made me excited. "Everybody in here is important to me, and has helped me along the way, giving me some type of feedback, guidance, or listening ear. I appreciate you all." Domino squeezed my hand and I smiled. "This is a pretty exciting season for me. Well, for Domino and I. He opened his second club location, I passed my state board exam, and we got engaged." I held up my hand, so everyone could admire the ring. I was in awe anytime I looked at it. "Now, I'm the owner of my very own salon, and I'm also about to embark on a new journey. Motherhood!"

Everyone in the crowd cheered and clapped. Some guests seemed surprised, while others seemed overly excited. There wasn't one dry eye in the room. Even my parents and Tasmine had smiles on their faces. I'd had my reservations about inviting them, but I was glad that I did. Their support was everything right now.

"Thank you, everyone! Now, let's party!" I cued the deejay to turn the music back up, and everyone flocked to me to tell me congratulations and to rub my stomach.

My sister pulled me away from the crowd, giving me the biggest hug she'd ever given me. "I love you so much, Bai."

"Thank you, Tasmine. Thank you for finally accepting him."

She laughed and wiped her eyes. "It's not that I didn't

accept him, Bailee. I knew he was mean in grade school, and I knew that he'd hurt Sapphire. But – "

"That's the thing, Tas. He didn't hurt Sapphire. Sapphire played him. I know she's your friend, but I believe his version of the story."

"Well, actually Sapphire isn't my friend anymore, because I told her I wasn't gonna break y'all up."

My eyes lowered, and my mouth dropped open. Tasmine nodded her head. "Bailee, all that shit I brought to you...the video of them dancing, the chick's Instagram page...all that was because Sapphire wanted me to prove to you that he wasn't shit, so you'd leave him. I finally found out it was because she was trying to get back with him."

"Did you know she was going to Miami?" I was curious, and wasn't in the mood to be lied to.

Tasmine shook her head. "I found out after the fact. That's when I started asking questions, and she admitted she wanted him to herself. I'm not sure if Domino is as bad as the picture she painted, but as long as he makes you happy, I'm okay."

"He does, Tas. I've never been so happy in my life."

We hugged again, and I continued to mingle with all the other guests. I couldn't believe how many of the invited guests had actually shown up, and I still couldn't believe I'd graduated and opened my own shop, all in one day. Today had been a great one, despite all my anxieties.

Chapter Twenty-Six
DEDRICK BLACK
The next day...

Bailee invited me to her graduation and grand opening yesterday, but I hadn't gone. I wasn't in the mood to be around people. All I'd wanted to do was sleep and play with chemicals. No human interaction. If it wasn't Venice, there was no need to converse. I'd send Bailee a congratulatory card through Domino. I know yesterday was her day, but I didn't feel like celebrating anything, and I didn't want to be the party pooper. My life had gone from sugar to sugar honey iced tea, and I was probably the blame for that. Had I not invited Brittany over to talk, Venice never would've ran into her at my house. And instead of being a part and miserable, we would've been together and happy.

God, I missed Venice. Every time I tried to call her, her phone went to voicemail. I'd filled up her voicemail with messages asking her to call me back, and hadn't even gotten a text back yet.

I understood why she was mad, but I just wished she'd hear me out. If she heard my explanation, she would know that Brittany being around twice was nothing more than a bad coincidence, and I could also try to persuade her that I was the man for her.

Instead of being in Venice's presence, I was in the lab at school, playing with two of my friends – Aluminum and Mercury. Usually, when I was in the lab, my brain was able to focus solely on science and chemistry, but today, I could barely mix the formula accurately because all I kept thinking about was Venice. Her face. Her eyes. Her breasts that were round like melons...melons on a hot summer day. Her laugh. Her interest in my chemicals, goals, and dreams...everything. No matter how many molecules I surrounded myself with, I couldn't stop thinking about how upset I was that Brittany showed up, scaring her off.

Speaking of Brittany. That little skank was staring at me from outside the door at the moment, but I threw my hoodie over my head and looked down, so I wasn't making eye contact with her.

"Dedrick! Are you gonna talk to me?" She yelled inside the classroom.

"The subscriber you are trying to reach is not interested in prostitutes." I sang, while mixing my formula. I never looked up at her, though. "Please leave."

"I'm sorry, Dedrick. I'm at a point where I'd...I'd do anything to have a nice guy like you. Teddy hurts me...badly."

"Well, now you know how I felt." I threw my hand up in the air. "Talk to the hand, 'cuz I am *not* your man." I learned that one from some teenagers at the library one day.

When Brittany turned around and walked out of the door, something in me decided it was time to go get Venice. I'd given her time to cool off, but she didn't seem like she'd be coming back on her own, so I wanted to go get her. Was I desperate? Heck yeah! You would be too if your soulmate walked out on you. She was the vanilla to my wafer and unless we were together, the taste wasn't right.

One hour later...
I'd gone to Venice's house, but she wasn't there. So, I decided to pull up to the daycare that her daughter, Sarai went to. She'd have to come here sooner or later, and when she did, I was going to beg her back. I couldn't imagine my life without her. She'd punished me enough, and I wasn't going to let her get away.

I didn't realize I'd drifted off to sleep, but what woke me was the tapping on the window. "What are you doing here, Dedrick?" It was Venice. I swear, she was as pretty as the city she was named after. Wearing an orange cardigan with black leggings and brown boots, her beautiful brown skin glistened under the November sun. I know my penis shouldn't have gotten erect, because this was nor the time or place, but that's just what Venice did to me.

Wiping the drool that had slid out of my mouth, I jumped up and opened the door. I was so excited that I accidentally hit Venice with it, causing her to fall to the ground. "I'm so sorry, Venice. I'm so sorry." I helped her up. "I never meant to hurt you."

As soon as I said that, she laughed. "Oh, well, you did a good job of that. But, I should've expected that from you. I mean, look at who your brothers are. And when we met, you said you didn't want a woman. So, it was my fault for wanting it to be more than it was."

She turned to walk in the daycare, but I grabbed her arm. "Please, Venice. I'm begging you. Here me out."

"You've got two minutes, Dedrick. Three minutes from now, I'll be late picking my daughter up, and whatever you have to say isn't worth the late fee."

I handed her all the cash I had balled up in my pocket, which equaled out to be only twenty-three dollars. Not much, but hopefully enough to keep her out her with me a few more minutes.

"I don't need this, Dedrick." She gave it back to me. "I need honesty. Who was that girl? Why'd she keep showing up? If she's really your ex, why can't she leave you alone? I told you that I got cheated on by my child's father, and here you go, doing the same damn thing!" Her voice rose and she began to cry, but I was thoroughly confused because we weren't technically in a relationship yet. Even though I'd love to be.

Suddenly, it hit me that the same way she felt about me, was how I felt about Brittany. And the last thing I wanted to do was treat her the way Brittany had treated me.

Wrapping my arms around her, I let her cry on my chest as I rubbed her back. "I'm so sorry, Dedrick. It's just...I have a lot going on right now. And I haven't been completely honest with you, either. I guess the guilt is killing me. I've been trying to stay away from you, so I wouldn't have to give you this news."

I felt a lump in my heart fall from my suspenders to my Chuck Taylors when she said that. All types of thoughts ran through my head. *Was she a prostitute like Brittany? Did she help her baby's father commit murder? Was he really not an ex? Did she really not like Dexter's Laboratory and Scooby-Doo as much as she'd claimed she had? Did she have an STD like Brittany?*

"What is it?" I blurted out as she continued to cry. My anxiety was getting the best of me, because I was assuming the worst. But even in the worst situation, I couldn't see myself wanting to let her go. She was too perfect to me.

"My ex...I...I have to...I have to tell you something."

"Venice, if you're still with him, just – "

"I'm not with him!" She shouted. "I'll never be with him again."

"Then, what's the problem, Venice?" I was confused. She was acting like she had something to say, but she was hesitant. "Is he out of jail and looking for me?" If so, I would just tell Domino. I doubted the few years I took martial arts would take out a man who'd spent time in jail for murder.

Venice shook her head, which gave me some comfort, because that meant he wasn't coming for me. At least not right now.

"Then what is it, sweetheart?" I asked, rubbing the small of her back.

"I just found this out, okay. And ever since I've found out, it's been tearing me up inside. I had no idea, Dedrick, and I'm so sorry. I swear I'm sorry." She shook her head frantically, letting the tears fly out. I hated seeing her this upset. And, she was making me nervous. I felt the gas bubbles in my stomach formulate.

I tried to calm her down, so I could in turn calm down. "Don't be sorry, Venice. Just talk to me. You had no idea that what? I'm a big boy; just tell me."

"Dedrick...my ex...he's the same guy who killed your parents!"

To be continued...

CPSIA information can be obtained
at www.ICGtesting.com
Printed in the USA
LVHW051559020819
626317LV00002B/410/P